Princesses' Night Out

...unexpectedly leads to their happy-ever-after!

Princesses Isabella and Francesca of Monterossa have always been inseparable—until now! As the king's health falters, their lives stand on the brink of irrevocable change, with Francesca's ascension to the throne drawing nearer. So when the twins find themselves in London for an official engagement, they decide to embrace one final adventure before surrendering to royal duty...

Only, Isabella stumbles upon her billionaire ex-fiancé, Rowan—and he's even more handsome than she remembers. But when they're caught in a misleadingly intimate moment, they have no choice but to chase the overzealous paparazzi into the city streets!

In *How to Win Back a Royal*
by Justine Lewis

And with her free-spirited sister gallivanting around London, Francesca enlists the help of her royal protection officer to track Isabella down. The very same bodyguard she's been harboring very off-limits feelings for!

In *Temptation in a Tiara*
by Karin Baine

Both available now!

Dear Reader,

When my fellow author Justine Lewis came up with the idea of writing about two princesses let loose for the night, I was immediately on board!

It was a lot of fun for me to write Francesca's night of freedom in London with her bodyguard, Giovanni. I hope you enjoy reading it just as much!

Lots of love,

Karin x

TEMPTATION IN A TIARA

KARIN BAINE

ROMANCE

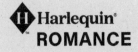

Harlequin®
ROMANCE

ISBN-13: 978-1-335-21638-0

Temptation in a Tiara

Copyright © 2025 by Karin Baine

Harlequin Enterprises ULC
22 Adelaide St. West, 41st Floor
Toronto, Ontario M5H 4E3, Canada
www.Harlequin.com

Printed in U.S.A.

Karin Baine lives in Northern Ireland with her husband, two sons and her out-of-control notebook collection. Her mother and her grandmother's vast collection of books inspired her love of reading and her dream of becoming a Harlequin author. Now she can tell people she has a *proper* job! You can follow Karin on X @karinbaine1 or visit her website for the latest news, karinbaine.com.

Books by Karin Baine

Harlequin Romance

Pregnant Princess at the Altar
Highland Fling with Her Boss
Cinderella's Festive Fake Date

Harlequin Medical Romance

Christmas North and South

Festive Fling with the Surgeon

Royal Docs

Surgeon Prince's Fake Fiancée
A Mother for His Little Princess

An American Doctor in Ireland
Midwife's One-Night Baby Surprise
Nurse's New Year with the Billionaire
Tempted by Her Off-Limits Boss

Visit the Author Profile page
at Harlequin.com for more titles.

For Dad x

**Praise for
Karin Baine**

"Emotionally enchanting! The story was fast-paced,
emotionally charged and oh so satisfying!"
—*Goodreads* on *Their One-Night Twin Surprise*

CHAPTER ONE

PRINCESS FRANCESCA DI MARZANO couldn't breathe. Despite Twilight being a rooftop bar, she felt caged in. Trapped. The pressure that had been building since the second she'd stood outside Westminster Abbey with her sister, Isabella, now crushing her ribs and lungs.

She tried to focus on the present. On the fabulous décor of the swanky bar. The huge canopies overhead to shelter patrons from sun or rain, and the trailing purple and white fake wisteria hanging from trellises dotted around the floor, made to catch the eye. As were the huge sofas for the comfort of the clientele, and private booths where VIPs could be seen but not approached. Not to mention the pink fountain in the centre of it all, which people congregated around with cocktails in hand. Yet, despite the opulence, and attention to detail to give the illusion of a vast open-air garden,

Francesca still felt as though she couldn't get enough oxygen into her body.

'Your Highness? Are you okay?' Giovanni Gallo, her royal protection officer, stopped to check on her, and Isabella disappeared into the crowd ahead.

If Francesca could've caught her breath, she would've called after her to stay close. She'd known this was a bad idea from the start, but her twin sister was the only person she felt close to in her life and it was difficult to say no to her. Even to something as hare-brained as ditching the evening celebrations the Duke of Oxford was hosting across the city in honour of the King of the United Kingdom's coronation. An event they were only attending to represent their father, who was currently recovering from his treatment for skin cancer at home in Monterossa.

Their homeland—a kingdom consisting of a group of islands and a small part of mainland Italy—couldn't be more different from the city of London. The very reason they'd wanted to explore it on their own terms.

Once they'd done their royal duty, it had been Isabella's idea to have one last night of fun, of trying to be normal, before Francesca possibly had to step into her father's role as monarch. She'd been preparing her whole life to become Queen, but now it was becoming a reality, she felt the pressure more than ever. Her father's cancer had spread into his lymph nodes, and, though they'd been removed, re-covery had taken longer than expected due to infection. There was a question mark hang-ing over his health, and whether or not he'd be fully fit to return to his duties. That meant the notion of Francesca, as next in line, becoming Queen was a strong possibility. A prospect that was seriously daunting.

However, freaking out in public was not the way to deal with it. She and Isabella had given the press enough juicy gossip to deal with over the years. Isabella's fiancé calling off their wedding shortly after he was pictured in a compromising position with two women on his stag night, followed by Francesca's failed engagement to Benigno last year, had given them more publicity than they could ever have wanted.

If she wasn't careful, Francesca was going to hand them more on a silver platter. Except, she couldn't seem to regulate her breathing.

'I. Can't. Breathe,' she gasped, clutching a hand to her chest. The pain indescribable.

Surely at twenty-nine years old she was too young to be having a heart attack?

Giovanni took her by the arm and guided her over to the side, away from everyone around them. But the thumping music reverberating through her whole body and the flashing lights were assaulting her senses. Not giving her the space she needed.

'Focus on me.' Giovanni held her by the shoulders, his deep, authoritative voice forcing her to look up at him.

He was at least a foot taller than her five-foot-four stature. An impressive figure. Staring at him wasn't a hardship either, and she did her best to focus on his big dark eyes.

'Deep breaths,' he insisted, placing her hand on his chest so she could feel the steady rise and fall as he inhaled.

She was focusing all right, but probably not on the things he was expecting her to. Francesca had harboured a crush on this particular member of the security team since he'd come on board four years ago. Although it was safe to say that, with his slicked-back black hair, stubble-lined sharp jaw, and impressive muscular build, most people who came in contact with him probably fancied the pants off him. Boxer briefs, she imagined...

Not that she had ever shared her impure thoughts about her bodyguard with anyone, not even her sister. It wouldn't be becoming of a future queen to contemplate a relationship with a member of staff. She was expected to marry someone of noble birth, even though that hadn't worked out so well for her so far. But Francesca always did the right thing when it came to her royal status. She did as she was told; did what was expected of her by her family and the country. What she wanted was never part of the equation.

Exactly why watching the British monarch's coronation had sent her into such a spin. Knowing that some day, probably soon, she was no longer going to be just Francesca, doing as she was told. From that moment on she would be Queen. With even greater expectations put upon her. Even the thought was enough for her to start gasping again and she had to focus on Giovanni, blocking out all thoughts, sights and sounds other than his handsome face.

'In…and out,' Giovanni instructed, and Francesca was compelled to follow until her breathing was gradually regulated back to normal.

'I thought I was dying,' she said eventually. Part of her wondered if that was wishful thinking. Then she wouldn't have to deal with the coronation or contemplate marriage to someone else she didn't love.

Benigno had been right when he'd called off their engagement, realising that she wasn't in it for the right reasons. But how could she ever marry for love when her country was the one thing that had her heart and her loyalty? Marriage for Francesca wasn't the romantic fantasy most grew up harbouring. From an early age she'd been told that it was her duty. She would marry because it was expected, and to someone deemed acceptable for the role of King alongside her. For no other reason.

Finding a soul mate, someone she'd be content to veg out with in front of the TV at night, wasn't a luxury she thought she could have. So she'd gone with Benigno as a viable option and tried to make it work, but apparently he had been hoping for that soul-mate connection. Now she was back at square one. In want of a husband. According to her parents, at least.

Her mother had even provided files on the eligible bachelors in attendance today, putting the emphasis on her finding a replacement for Benigno soon.

This wasn't the first time Francesca wished that those five minutes between her birth and

Isabella's had been the other way around. Her twin sister at least didn't have quite the same worries as she had, and might actually be able to marry for love. She'd already come close to marrying a commoner. And yes, their father, King Leopold, had married Gloria Gold, an actress, but that had been a scandal too. Francesca didn't want her reign to start with any more black marks against her. Besides, she was running out of time on that front too.

It would be preferable for her to already have married by the time she was crowned so that her love life was not the main topic of conversation surrounding her reign. A nice marriage of convenience between her and someone suitable, arranged by royal advisors, would save a lot of time when she could spend a lifetime searching for someone able to capture a piece of her heart. Something that wasn't going to help her position any.

'A panic attack. Not surprising when you and your sister are out in public without the usual security team. You know when you attend anything we usually put weeks of planning in first to assess any risk...' It was clear Giovanni was ticked off at her for putting them both in this situation, but at least no harm had been done. Perhaps she should take his advice before something did happen that would put them in danger. The last thing she wanted was for anyone to get hurt, or her parents to have cause for concern.

'I know. This was a stupid idea. We'll get Isabella and go back before anyone notices.' Even better, they could just go back to their hotel and forget this ever happened.

'Are you feeling better?' Giovanni didn't take his eyes off her and Francesca felt the air go from her lungs again.

She swallowed hard. 'Yes.'

Once he seemed satisfied that she wasn't going to pass out on him, he let go of her shoulders. 'Okay. We'll get Isabella and go.'

Francesca nodded, happy for him to take charge. This had all been very exciting in theory, but the reality was too much. She'd spent so much of her life being told where to go and how to act that being left to her own devices was overwhelming. Like one of those caged animals whipped into submission that, even when they were released from captivity, still paced the small path they were used to.

Francesca wouldn't even know what to do with a life of her own.

Giovanni took her by the hand and they walked towards the bar. She might've been tempted to sample the rainbow wall of brightly coloured bottles if she weren't already feeling sick. It wasn't how she'd imagined tonight going. When Isabella had first suggested it, Francesca had pictured dancing and cocktails, and not the formal dancing expected at functions. Real cutting loose on the dance floor.

Although that didn't seem to be the norm here either. Most people were just milling about, drinks in hand, probably trying to find a hook-up for the evening. Something else she wouldn't know anything about. It occurred to her that, for an almost thirty-year-old woman, there were an awful lot of life experiences she hadn't had the opportunity to explore. However, tonight was not going to be the night for that either, when at the first whiff of freedom she'd gone into a tailspin.

'Can you see her anywhere?' Giovanni was straining to see around the bar area.

Francesca looked for the siren-red outfit her sister had chosen for this evening. Although she'd deemed it a bit too eye-catching for someone who needed to stay under the radar, it should help them find her in this crowded area. Except she was nowhere to be seen. As they moved around the rooftop with increasing urgency, Francesca couldn't help but worry.

'I'll check the ladies' bathroom,' she suggested when it became clear that her sister was not in the immediate vicinity.

'I'll check first.' Giovanni prepared to swing into bodyguard mode, his hand on the door before Francesca could go in.

'I thought we were trying not to draw attention to ourselves.' Although it was protocol for him to scout out everywhere she went first, this was taking it to extremes.

Giovanni nodded and agreed with some reluctance. 'At least let me keep the door open so I can respond as quickly as possible if something happens.'

She wasn't going to argue, knowing this was seriously testing his need to control everything, and let him hold the door open with his foot whilst she checked the cubicles.

Apart from a couple of young women chatting at the washbasins there was no one else inside.

'Excuse me? You haven't seen my sister anywhere, have you?' Francesca approached, showing them the photo on her phone that she'd taken of Isabella just before they'd left the hotel.

'We passed her on our way in downstairs a few minutes ago.'

'Oh, yeah. I saw her leave with some guy on a scooter.'

The blood in Francesca's veins chilled at the thought that her sister had just taken off into the night in a strange city without even telling her.

'Was she struggling? Did she go against her will?' Giovanni pushed his way inside to interrogate the stunned women.

'Giovanni, I don't think this is the place—' Despite her urgency to find her sister, Francesca was still aware of causing a scene.

'Was she upset? Who took her?' He dismissed her concerns to continue his line of questioning.

The women blinked at him for some time before answering, probably trying to process the fact there was a handsome six-foot-plus man in here.

'She seemed okay.'

'I wasn't paying that much attention. I was more worried about getting past the bouncers. Did you see the bald one checking my ID?' The redhead giggled to her blonde friend, and it was clear they'd had other things on their minds besides the stranger they'd passed on the way in.

Francesca supposed it was good that neither she nor Isabella had been recognised at least.

'You must remember something,' Giovanni insisted.

Francesca put her hand on his arm. 'I think we should probably go.'

Her attempt to persuade him to drop this before they did draw attention seemed to work when he sighed, his shoulders dropping as he took his leave, Francesca joining him.

'So she's not here and doesn't seem to have been taken against her will. It wouldn't be beyond Isabella to decide to go off on her own. Why don't we go outside where I can hear myself think and I'll give her a call?' Hopefully she could tell her how silly she was being and persuade her to come back before any damage was done.

'What about the geolocator on her phone?'

Francesca flushed pink. 'We turned those off. We didn't want anyone to know where we were going.'

In her defence, she hadn't realised she'd lose her sister within five minutes of having their freedom.

'You girls will be the death of me,' Giovanni muttered under his breath as he led the way back out of the building.

It made Francesca smile to see the usual cool and collected bodyguard show his frustration. So, he was human after all. Sometimes she wondered, when he seemed as emotionless as she was accused of being at times.

'Well, don't plan on dying until we're all safe and sound back at the hotel.' She batted her eyelashes at him, ignoring the serious side eye he gave her.

Such was the nature of their relationship. A back and forth where she made him subtly aware it annoyed the hell out of her having a shadow everywhere she went, and he tried to get her to take her security seriously.

Though tonight she was sorry she hadn't taken his advice for once when he'd told them both in no uncertain terms, when he'd caught them sneaking out of the party at the Ashton in Mayfair, that this was a bad idea.

'The first thing we should do is try and contact her.' At least Giovanni was thinking clearly. Francesca needed him to teach her how to be so calm in a crisis. A skill she was going to need sooner rather than later. It was fine when she had everyone doing everything for her, dressing her, planning her day, advising her on what matters she'd be dealing with, but becoming Queen was going to require more independent thinking and a strength she apparently had yet to find.

Francesca pulled her small phone from her diamanté clutch bag, which didn't hold much else beyond her lipstick and her hairbrush, but she was glad to have something practical to do.

She pulled up her list of contacts and tapped on her sister's icon. She waited to connect, but the call was put straight through to voicemail.

'I'll send her a text in case she's somewhere she can't hear her phone.' Francesca waited, hoping for a response, but none came.

'Where would she go?' Giovanni had clearly moved to the next phase, which she suspected would include them scouring the city to find Isabella. Something Francesca had hoped to avoid, but it looked as though this wasn't going to be wrapped up so easily.

She could only blink at Giovanni in response. She had no idea where Isabella had gone, or why. More importantly, Isabella hadn't confided in her about what she was doing. If she'd gone of her own volition, it implied she hadn't wanted Francesca to know the answer to any of those questions. Suggesting it wasn't going to be anything she would approve of. Courting trouble they certainly didn't need.

It made her wonder if this had been her

sister's plan after all. If her proposal for this evening had had nothing to do with Francesca having one night of normality, and more about giving Isabella the chance to sneak away and do whatever she wanted. The moment she knew for sure her sister was all right, Francesca was going to kill her.

'Think, Francesca. Who does she know in London?' Giovanni knew they were all in serious trouble. He'd taken his eye off the ball. Let his fondness for the Princesses override his common sense and, more importantly, protocol. Now he was solely responsible for whatever happened to Isabella and Francesca, and with one of them missing, it didn't bode well.

'She doesn't know anybody.' Francesca's big amber eyes were full of worry. It was clear she was struggling to focus on the matter at hand, concern for her sister overriding everything else.

Giovanni knew how they close they were. They did everything together, and he was sure right now it felt as though Francesca were missing a limb. However, he needed her to be her usual strong self. He'd seen her deal with some tough stuff in the years he'd been employed at the palace, her petite frame belying the strength of character within that he so admired. She was going to make a good queen when the time came. He just had to do his job as well and make sure to get both her and Isabella safely home.

'Does she talk to anyone online? Has she met anyone from the UK before? There must be someone she knows in the country.' Although it seemed as though he were putting all the responsibility on Francesca right now, he knew he was the one who'd fallen short in his duties.

As an ex-soldier, he should have known to keep his eyes, and his mind, on the targets at all times. The last time he'd been distracted, his army buddies had been hurt. He prayed his neglect wouldn't have the same outcome here. Not only for his sake, but for Isabella's, and Francesca's too. He was already carrying enough guilt over hurting people close to him, without causing the royal family more distress.

The whole reason he'd taken this position was to atone for those he'd hurt in the past. Becoming a royal protection officer, bodyguard to the Princesses, was the ultimate way to pay back to his country. His job was his life with no room for relationships outside the one he had with his employers. He'd hoped that meant no one ever getting close enough to end up hurt again. Only time would tell if he'd managed that.

Though this was a job where he couldn't afford to make any mistakes. One slip-up could mean Francesca's safety being compromised. Not only was she the future Queen, but also someone he'd become very fond of.

Something he'd done his best to ignore, hoping that any affection he felt towards her was temporary. That it would fizzle out the longer he was in the job, getting to know the person beyond the tiara. Except it hadn't worked out that way. If anything, spending more time with Francesca had only made him admire her more.

She was devoted to her position in the royal family, and didn't take anything for granted. In his previous security work he'd dealt with other privileged people who had a tendency to be self-centred, thinking only of their own wants and needs. The opposite to how Francesca conducted herself. It took something special to be so focused and carry the weight of responsibility she did without complaint. He should know.

So it was natural he should be impressed by someone so beautiful inside and out. Her flawless olive skin, perfect plump lips, and the tumbling dark waves of hair falling to her shoulders made her look like the perfect fairy-tale princess. But she was so much more than her looks. He was attracted to her strength of spirit as much as her curvy little body.

It wasn't until she'd got engaged to Benigno that Giovanni had realised his feelings for her went beyond admiration. He'd never thought it a suitable match. Francesca needed someone as strong as she was, who was capable of supporting her once she became Queen. That wasn't Benigno and it had frustrated Giovanni no end to think of her tying herself to him for the rest of her days. Apart from anything else, there hadn't been a spark between them. Not like the one Giovanni and Francesca had. Even though he was far from suitable either. He'd been glad when the wedding was called off, sure that Francesca would get over the initial hurt in time, and he'd been right. It didn't mean she wouldn't find another partner he'd find difficult to see her going out with.

However, he was a professional too, and Francesca's safety had to be his priority over any feelings that could come to nothing.

When Francesca didn't answer his question, he had to refrain from shaking her. Royal protocol dictated that he shouldn't touch her unless it was in the line of duty, guiding her out of harm's way. Which probably wasn't a bad thing in the circumstances. He needed to keep some emotional distance. 'In that case, I'm going to have to call this in as a security alert and we're going to have to let the police deal with it.'

Something he was reluctant to do when it was sure to cause an incident large enough for the royal family to hear about. So much for the discreet night out the girls had promised before he'd agreed to this craziness…

'Please don't do that, Gio.' Francesca grabbed his arm, her full pink lips pleading with him. 'As far as we know, she went willingly with someone. We just have to find her. If we alert the security forces this whole thing is going to escalate and it's the last thing my family needs right now.'

Giovanni was torn between doing exactly what he knew he should, and the Princess calling him Gio, asking for his help. And touching him, making it personal. For once, he let his heart rule his head. 'Well, we're going to need somewhere to start. London's a big city.'

Francesca thought for a moment. Then those big eyes grew even wider with that childlike enthusiasm he saw in her every time she was on a royal engagement meeting new people.

'Oh. I think she stayed in touch with that pop star, Leanne. You know, the one with the baby-pink hair and star tattoos on her face.'

'Is she the one who sang that weird whispery song with the bells?' He wasn't up to date with the latest music, he had more important things to think about, but he remembered Isabella playing it over and over again in the car. Whispering barely heard lyrics accompanied by handbells wasn't his idea of music, but she was apparently popular.

'Yeah. She was supposed to play at Isabella's wedding.' Even the mention of the doomed wedding made Francesca flinch.

It had been a big tabloid headline when Isabella's fiancé had been photographed cavorting with other women on his stag do. Swiftly followed by another announcing the end of the relationship only days before the wedding. It had been a nightmare all around, not only for Isabella and her family, but for the palace PR department, and those who'd had to inform all of the dignitaries who were supposed to be attending the event.

'What about the ex? Are you sure she's not with him?' It wouldn't be unheard of for someone to get back with their ex, even though he personally hadn't ever done that. He took a casual approach to relationships and made sure the women he hooked up with realised that. Then no one got hurt.

Francesca shook her head. 'As far as I know Isabella hasn't spoken to Rowan since everything happened.'

'What makes you think this Leanne might be a good lead? Do you know where she is?'

'I know she's hosting her own party in the city tonight, not far from here.' Francesca shrugged.

It was as good a shout as any, he supposed. 'Okay. We'll head there and you keep trying Isabella on the way.'

Giovanni at least had a plan, somewhere to start. Usually he preferred to work with a lot more information, but this whole mess was his own fault. He just hoped he was the only one who'd suffer the consequences of his bad decision-making this time.

CHAPTER TWO

FRANCESCA SHOWED GIOVANNI the address of the club where Leanne was hosting her coronation party, praying this was a one-stop fix.

'Should we get a taxi?' Usually, she didn't have to worry about transport—someone always arranged that for her. She was aware of her privilege, but it had never really been an issue for her until now, when it became apparent she didn't really know how to function in the real world, never having to arrange anything herself. The royal family had people who did everything for them.

Thank goodness for Giovanni, one of the few people she knew who had experience of reality outside the palace walls. This might not be his country of birth either, but at least he knew how to get stuff done. A soldier who'd seen action knew how to survive a lot tougher situations than this.

The romantic fantasy of being in the city

alone was a lot scarier in person when she didn't know anyone here, or how to get around. It made her wonder how on earth she and Isabella had thought they could do this themselves. Though her sister took more risks—the perks of being the second born—she had no more real-life experience than Francesca.

The thought of the two of them wandering around this bustling city without a clue made her shudder. At least she had Giovanni to hold her hand. Wait…he was literally holding her hand and leading her down the street. She yanked her hand out of his grip, refusing to let him trail her any further. Okay, so she was at his mercy, but that didn't mean he got to take liberties with her. Not with something as intimate as hand-holding.

He must've seen the fury on her face at his impertinence when he turned to see why she'd stopped. Except instead of an apology, he was smirking.

'Listen, Princess, you're going to want to hold my hand before you get lost on the underground.'

'What are you talking about?'

'The Tube. You have heard of it? It's the quickest and easiest way to get about this city, otherwise we're going to waste time sitting in traffic.'

She hated that he was right, but that wasn't the only thing bothering her. 'Of course I've heard of it, but it'll be full of…people.'

His grin grew even more smug. 'Commoners, you mean? You're going to have to get used to it, Princess. You wanted to be normal for the night. That means being herded into too hot, too cramped, germ-ridden public transport instead of your golden carriage. This is how the other half actually lives.'

Although the concept was alien to her, she couldn't afford to be snobbish about getting on a train with the British public. She was the one who'd agreed with Isabella that going incognito would be a good idea, so she couldn't expect any special treatment. If they were going to keep this whole mess from their parents, she was going to have to blend in as best she could.

'Do you think I'm going to fit in?' It was one thing coming directly to the bar from the party in a car Giovanni had insisted on arranging upon hearing of their escape plan, but an entirely different story mixing with the public and hoping she wouldn't be recognised.

Giovanni looked her up and down and clicked his tongue. 'Hmm… Now you mention it you are a tad overdressed. We don't want to draw any more attention than the average pretty woman.'

Francesca stood patiently awaiting instruction, trying not to get too hung up on the fact that he'd called her pretty. Giovanni wasn't one for dishing out compliments. If anything, she thought him immune to her charms when, no matter what occasion or outfit, she never raised as much as a smile in response. Not that his appreciation was her goal when she was getting ready...

'Well, what do you suggest?' She folded her arms in defence against the things he was making her feel.

'This, for a start.'

She was tempted to back away when he reached out to her, afraid to let him touch her again, but she remained steadfast. Her heart beating frantically as he unpinned her hair from its sleek confines, letting her tresses fall freely around her shoulders.

Then he moved so close her face was almost buried in his chest as he undid the diamond and sapphire necklace around her neck. She could feel his breath on her cheek, smell the spicy scent of his cologne, and she had to force herself not to react.

'Put that in your bag.' His voice sounded more gruff than usual and she followed his command as he backed away.

Still, he wasn't done. He bent down and grabbed the tiered hem of her long cobalt-blue, off-the-shoulder silk dress, yanking until he managed to rip away one ruffle, then another. Leaving her feeling half naked now her body was exposed from the knees down.

'What the hell are you doing, Gio?' Never mind that he'd just shredded a very expensive designer dress, but his fingers were grazing some very intimate places in the process.

'There. Now you look like you're going clubbing, and not to a formal ball.' He looked so pleased with himself as he deposited the torn remnants of her dress into the nearest bin, Francesca thought he needed taking down a peg or two before he became unbearable.

'Well, you could do with some styling yourself if you want to blend in.' Now it was her turn to make him feel uncomfortable. Francesca undid his tie and slipped it from around his neck.

'Put that in your pocket,' she demanded in a tone not dissimilar to the one he'd used with her. Then she opened a couple of his shirt buttons, along with the one on his jacket.

'You could probably lose that altogether, you know. And roll your sleeves up.' Okay, so that was just a kink of hers, but he had lovely tanned, thick forearms and it was a shame to keep them hidden.

'Are you done now?' he asked sardonically.

'I guess.' Francesca shrugged, not giving anything away about how much she'd enjoyed stripping off some of his clothes with him standing helplessly, letting her do it. The frisson of power had at least taken her mind off her sister for a little while.

Wordlessly, he took her hand again and led her towards the underground station. She followed him down the steps and into a bustling hall full of commuters coming and going all around her. Francesca clung a little closer to her protector. He waved a card at one of the small barriers and passed through, but when Francesca approached it wouldn't budge. She tried again to push through it.

Noticing her absence, Giovanni turned and sighed. 'Use your credit card. You have to pay, Princess.'

'I don't have a credit card,' she muttered through gritted teeth. Despite the family having a lot of money, they had very little to do with it in reality.

'Oh, yeah. I forgot you people don't actually carry anything with you. Just how far did you and Isabella think you were going to get on charm and looks alone?' He pulled his wallet from the jacket he was carrying and took out another credit card, scanning it on her side of the barrier so she could get through and join him.

'I guess we didn't think things through.' Francesca felt her face grow hot with shame, embarrassed that they hadn't even thought about money. They were so used to having everything done for them they never had to pay anyone directly for anything. She'd taken her life of privilege for granted, never having to think about the practicalities of everyday living like everyone else.

'I guess not, Princess. Thank goodness I caught you both when I did. You hadn't even organised any transport, for goodness sake.' He shook his head, furthering her embarrassment when he clearly thought she was nothing but an airhead, and she had yet to prove otherwise to him.

'Do you think you could stop calling me that? I thought we were trying not to draw attention.' It was the only comeback she had.

'Princess? It's not in deference to your title. It's more...'

'An insult?'

'A term of endearment.'

They spoke over one another, but Francesca suspected her explanation was the truth. He thought her nothing but a spoiled, pampered princess, in every meaning of the word. What was worse than that was the realisation that it was true.

'I can't help the world I was born into, Giovanni. Yes, it comes with privileges most people aren't lucky enough to experience, but it isn't always a bed of roses being part of the royal family.'

'I know that, Francesca. I see you. I see how dedicated you are to your role.'

'Okay, then.' She decided to let the matter drop before he paid her any more compliments, letting her see a softer side of Giovanni that she wasn't used to.

'Okay, then.' He smiled and led the way over to the downward escalator leading to the train platforms.

When she faltered at the top of the moving stairway, he took her hand and urged her on with him.

'You have to stand on the right-hand side,' he told her.

Francesca bristled, and disentangled her fingers from his. 'I think I know how to stand on a step.'

It was one thing letting him guide her in this unfamiliar world, but he wasn't the boss of her. He had to remember his place.

'Excuse me.'

'Move.'

'You're supposed to stand on the right so people can pass on the left,' he repeated.

A stream of seemingly angry commuters pushed past her, knocking her into Giovanni. Forcing him once again to come to her rescue. He grabbed her around the waist, his big hands almost completely encircling her body, and transported her effortlessly onto the step in front of him. On the right.

'It's a stupid rule,' she fumed, not even looking back to see his smirk.

When they reached the bottom of the escalator they were faced with two signs and on this occasion she was happy to let Giovanni point her in the right direction. The platform wasn't too crowded and she stood patiently waiting for the train, which, according to the board, was due imminently.

She looked down at the dusty tracks, marvelling at the great feat of engineering providing links to the whole city and beyond. It occurred to her too that the location would make a great setting for a horror movie. Long, dark tunnels, and the Victorian-style architecture, made the thought of a creature hiding in the shadows entirely possible. So when she saw a little mouse scamper along, right in front of her, she let out a shriek and jumped straight into Giovanni's strong arms.

'It's all right. He won't come anywhere near you. He's just looking for food and somewhere quiet to rest.' Giovanni's voice was soft and soothing in her ear, and for a brief moment she thought about him whispering sweet nothings instead.

This was the problem. Giovanni was paid to be her protector, and, in turn, he made her feel like a fragile princess. When she was with him it was the only time she didn't have to be strong, make decisions, and pretend she was holding it together. Giovanni was always there to look after her; to see the real Francesca behind the royal front she had to adopt for the cameras and the general public. He made her feel safe, and, well, like a woman rather than a title.

She would have been content to stay in his arms the rest of the night, except a waft of cold air, a roar in the tunnel, and the glare of head-lights announced the arrival of the train.

'Hold my hand.' He didn't have to ask her twice.

As the doors opened, everyone on the plat-form swarmed forward, barely waiting for those on board to disembark before shoving their way onto the train. Francesca was car-ried on board in the wave of people, her feet barely touching the ground. Giovanni was her lifeline, holding her hand to keep her with him.

By the time the doors shut, she was pressed tightly up against him again, with no one pay-ing them any more attention than anyone else. Strange that this uncomfortable experience was the most chilled she'd been for a while. Francesca was used to people doing things for her, and telling her what to do. But it wasn't that often she got to switch off that royal per-sona. Didn't have to be on guard, watching everything she said or did. The circumstances she'd found herself in tonight weren't ideal, and she hoped Isabella was okay, but she was enjoying this little piece of freedom. As long as Giovanni was here to guide her through it.

The train jolted as it pulled away from the platform and she struggled to find her balance, grabbing Giovanni's shirt in her hand so she didn't fall.

'You might need to hold onto something else,' he growled, taking her hand and moving it from his chest to the bright yellow pole she was standing next to.

'Sorry.' She took a step back, embarrassed by her own neediness tonight.

'You're like an alien, you know.' At least he was smiling at her now, instead of that scowl he'd worn only moments ago. Even if he was insulting her.

'Pardon me?'

'It's like you've just been beamed down onto another planet from the mother ship. Everything's so new and bewildering to you.'

'Sorry I'm so annoying.' It seemed as though she was apologising a lot simply for being her tonight.

'No. Not at all. It's endearing when I'm so cynical about everything these days.' Giovanni didn't expand on his reasons for that, and Francesca had to wait until they were off the train and through the exit barriers before she could quiz him.

Walking out into the city again was another assault on the senses. There were so many people. Usually there was a barrier between her and the rest of the world, so it was no wonder she had some anxiety. Giovanni was right about everything being new and bewildering to her, but it was also terrifying.

She'd been wrapped in a bubble her whole life. One that she'd mostly resented but had no choice but to accept. It was her life to be a princess and then a queen some day, so of course she wasn't going to live like everyone else. She wondered how Isabella was coping with the change. Although they'd done everything together growing up, there had always been a certain distinction made between them because one of them was going to be Queen eventually, and one of them wasn't. Perhaps this life would be easier for Isabella to get used to when she didn't have the same pressure as their father's successor to the throne.

'What did you do before coming to the palace?' she asked, once they were away from the crowds and she had some personal space again.

'I was in the army.' Giovanni kept walking, facing straight ahead, giving nothing away.

She'd always been curious about him. The man behind the suit. But she'd always been careful to keep that emotional distance between them when they both had roles to fulfil, duties to carry out. Tonight had changed everything. At least for her. She'd had to let those defences down, put herself in his hands, and let him see her vulnerabilities. It seemed only fair she should know a little about him in return.

'Hmm, I could picture that.' Too well. Now she had an image of him in khaki, smeared with dirt and sweat...

'Not as glamorous as you probably imagine.'

Francesca blushed, even though he couldn't see her. 'How come you ended up at the palace, then?'

'We were on a peacekeeping mission and my unit was caught up in a clash with locals protesting an election. A lot of men got hurt and I left shortly after that.' He was very abrupt, giving little away, but Francesca was determined to get to know something about him.

'Were you medically discharged, then?' She wondered what hidden injuries he'd sustained when he looked like the fittest man she'd ever met.

'Not me, but I decided I'd had enough. Shouldn't you try Isabella again?' It was obvious he was trying to change the subject as he kept walking, with Francesca tottering on her heels trying to keep up with his fast pace.

'If you weren't injured, why did you leave?'

Francesca typed out another text message to her sister as she talked.

Giovanni stopped so abruptly she nearly ran into the back of him. His shoulders sagged as he heaved out a sigh.

'Because it was my fault. I was the captain, making decisions and responsible for operations. I hadn't realised the depth of political unrest. Riot gear and barbed wire obviously were no match for the incendiary devices that had been planted at the buildings we were defending. My failure to plan, and keep my team safe, changed people's lives for ever.'

'But you didn't plant any bombs. You didn't go out with the intention of hurting your friends.' It seemed clear-cut to her. Even though she knew what guilt felt like, warranted or not.

When Benigno had called off the wedding, she'd hated the scandal it had caused her family. Regardless that it hadn't been her doing. Although her parents hadn't been physically wounded, like Giovanni's army mates, they'd been hurt by the shame the broken engagement had brought to their door. And nothing anyone said or did could ever lessen the guilt she carried over that. Something she apparently had in common with her bodyguard.

Giovanni, however, didn't have her parents'

disapproval hanging over every action and decision. Francesca had learned from an early age that she had to truly earn her parents' approval, and that meant failure wasn't an option in any area of her life. A difficult concept for a young child to accept, but she'd realised quickly that her parents' love came with conditions.

Never stepping out of line, never talking back, getting dirty, or making any kind of mistake in public. It seemed she wasn't worthy of love unless she was perfect.

Isabella had a different relationship with them. Although she had her own challenges, they seemed to make more allowances where she was concerned. Probably because she wasn't scrutinised just as much as the future Queen. Their mother and father had been sympathetic to them after their respective break-ups. To a point. Francesca couldn't help but feel as though she'd failed them in some way when Benigno had called off their engagement. She'd been more gutted about that than the end of her relationship. It felt to her as though it represented a flaw in her character. Something her parents wouldn't have appreciated. She desperately didn't want to disappoint them again.

'I let it happen. That's as good as detonating the bomb in my book.' All traces of soft

Giovanni disappeared, leaving behind the steely voiced, fast-walking version.

'Can you slow down? I'm in heels, and they're killing me.' They were only meant for show. It was very rare she had to walk very far in this kind of garb, and exactly the reason she and Isabella carried their 'emergency shoes'. Little ballet-slipper flats, which fitted into their bags. Isabella's bag tonight, as it happened.

Giovanni suddenly did a one-hundred-and-eighty-degree turn and dropped down to her feet. He lifted one shoe off the ground and pulled it off her foot. Francesca had to lean on him so she didn't fall over. Giovanni moved to her other foot, leaving her standing barefoot on the pavement.

He took both shoes, walked over to the small wall lining the footpath, and banged both shoes hard until the heels snapped off. Francesca could only watch open-mouthed.

'There,' he said, handing back her mutilated stilettos. 'Flats. You're welcome.'

'Have you any idea how much those shoes are worth?' Her voice was at a pitch capable of shattering nearby windows.

'Have you?'

Touché.

Francesca let that one go, knowing he was

just trying to rile her because she'd elicited some personal information from him.

'It's not healthy to hold onto that guilt, you know. Especially when you did nothing wrong.' She should know.

She felt bad, not only about what her parents had gone through, but also because Benigno had been right. She had been closed off from him. Such was the way she'd been brought up as the future Queen—not to show her emotions, and to put all her energy into maintaining her public persona. Though that part hadn't worked out so well.

It wasn't only her parents she didn't want to hurt again. She had no intention of marrying anyone who didn't know the score from the outset. A marriage at this stage was going to have to be something arranged by two families. More of a business transaction between two parties, then her future husband wouldn't be expecting something she couldn't give him. Love. Apparently she reserved that only for her country, and her responsibility to her position in the royal family.

'It's my fault people I loved got hurt, and not for the first time.' He muttered the last bit as he stomped away, but Francesca had caught it and it left her wondering what else he was holding back.

As they rounded the corner, they almost walked straight into the crowd standing outside the club.

'Wait.' Giovanni shot out a hand and stopped her from going any further. 'There are photographers waiting.'

'Of course there are. Why didn't I think of that?' This was a celebrity party. Wherever there was a collection of famous people, there would inevitably be press waiting, ready to capture unflattering pictures. What on earth would her parents think if they saw her stumbling into a club in her ripped outfit?

'You stay here. I'll go and make sure your name is on that list for admittance.'

'What if they see me here?'

'They're waiting for limos. The last thing they'll expect is a princess on foot.' He gave a pointed look at her ruined shoes. 'Just stay back. Let me handle this.'

Francesca had no other choice.

Giovanni rolled down his sleeves, put his tie and jacket on, and did his best to look like the professional he was supposed to be. Somewhere along the way tonight he'd forgotten that, sharing details of his personal life, and getting way too close to Francesca physically and emotionally.

At least when he was back in his proper role in public he might be able to put some of that professional distance between them again. All he had to do was slip Francesca discreetly into the club, where they'd hopefully find Isabella. Having two princesses to look after again was infinitely better than one, when it would take his mind off every touch he'd shared with Francesca tonight in pursuit of her wayward sister.

He'd had plenty of experience getting his clients into venues discreetly, and no one challenged him as he strode through the throng of people and straight to the security detail at the club door.

He explained he had a royal princess requesting admittance, and after some conflab over walkie-talkies, Francesca's name was added to the party list. Leanne was apparently thrilled to have her in attendance. Now all he had to do was get Francesca inside without any photographic evidence that could end up in tomorrow's gossip columns.

He walked back up to where he'd left her.

'Well?' she asked, taking a short break from biting her French-manicured nails.

'They couldn't tell me if Isabella's in there, it's possible she's under a fake name, but they have agreed to letting you in. They had to contact Leanne for permission so I'm afraid we can't just walk in, take a look and leave. You'll probably have to say hello at least.'

'Okay, but how am I going to get in there without being seen?'

'You're probably not going to like it...' Giovanni stripped off his jacket and held it above her head.

'No, but I trust you.'

He knew that was a big deal for Francesca. In her position there weren't a lot of people she could trust. It meant a lot to him too, even though it was a huge responsibility to keep her safe. Especially in these circumstances.

'Keep into the shadows until we get near, jacket over your head, and pressed close to me so no one can see your face.'

She nodded, though he could see the apprehension on her face. More pressure on him to get this right.

With the feel of Francesca's hands pressed tight through his shirt, branding his skin, he pushed his way inside the club. Determined to protect her at all costs.

It didn't matter the life-or-death situations

he'd been in countless times before, or that this was just about dodging the press, his heart was still pounding, sweat breaking on his skin, knowing he had to keep her safe. She trusted him. Just as his parents had. Just as his army unit had.

Once inside, Francesca let go, and handed him his jacket back. Her eyes were shining, her smile wide, almost as though she'd enjoyed the exhilaration of the moment. 'We did it.'

'Let's hope so,' he muttered, hoping none of this would come back to bite them on the backside. Isabella had a lot to answer for.

This place was definitely not his scene. There was a seventies disco floor, which lit up as people walked on it and was nearly as bright as the strobe lights flashing all around. Then there were the life-size leopards posed between potted palms along the edge of the room. The word tacky came to mind, but it probably cost more to decorate this area than he earned in a year. It was true that money couldn't buy taste. Or perhaps he too was becoming used to the finer things in life at the palace, where everything was tasteful and elegant. The contrast between the two worlds never more evident than when the hostess of the party came to greet them.

Leanne, a petite, pink-haired teen, dressed in some kind of silver-foil bikini and fishnet tights, was the opposite to the demure appearance of Princess Francesca, whom he'd had to customise just to blend in with this crowd. Though he knew which look he preferred...

'Your Highness. I can't believe you're actually here.'

Leanne attempted a curtsey but was quickly discouraged by Francesca.

'There's no need for formalities. Just call me Francesca.'

'You have to meet everyone.' Social etiquette now out of the window, she grabbed Francesca and rushed her through to the party hub.

With leopard-print-clad drag queens wandering amongst the partygoers with trays of smoking cocktails, and half-naked men wearing crowns, handing out plastic tiaras, Giovanni thought he'd walked into someone's fever dream.

'I don't want the press to know I'm here. I'm supposed to be at an official function.' Francesca had to yell over the music to be heard, which mocked any idea of secrecy.

'It's fine. I've banned phones. You're safe.' Keen to show off her new best friend, Leanne dragged Francesca onto the middle of the dance floor.

So much for keeping a low profile. As the girls danced, Giovanni stood on sentry duty, scouting the room, not only for potential threats, but also for cameras.

'I hope you don't mind us crashing your party.' Francesca cosied up to their gracious host.

'Not at all. I'm thrilled to have an actual royal in attendance.'

Giovanni did wonder if Leanne knew Francesca wasn't a member of the British royal family...

'It's so much more fun than the one we were supposed to be attending. I was wondering if you'd seen my sister, Isabella?' Francesca was doing all the right things, flattering her host, and not making a big deal about her sister's disappearance.

'Does your bodyguard have to stand so close? He's kind of killing the vibe.' Leanne glared at him like a petulant child who always got what she wanted. Which didn't include a sensible adult.

'It's my job,' he told her, folding his arms and planting his feet firmly on the sticky floor.

Leanne grabbed one of the sparkly silver tiaras from a nearby drag queen and perched it on his head. 'There, that's better.'

Francesca was smirking. 'It does kind of suit you.'

'I think it would look much better on you, Princess.' He took it off and carefully placed it on her head, making her look like the princess she was in a room full of pretenders.

She smiled at him. 'Maybe you could take a step back, Giovanni. I think I'm safe enough here.'

'Yeah, Gio, go chill with the other stiffs.' Leanne nodded towards the edge of the floor where there was a bank of similar-looking imposing male figures. No doubt security for the other rich and famous attendees who thought looking good on the dance floor was more important than staying safe.

The one thing that irked him more than being dismissed by this precocious pop princess was her using the nickname only real royalty got to use. He looked at Francesca to see what she wanted him to do. She nodded, giving him a look of apology, and he knew she was only doing this to get closer to Leanne.

Reluctantly, he took to the sidelines as he heard Francesca ask again about her sister.

He and the other security gave each other a

nod of acknowledgement, but when he spotted a familiar face he couldn't help but let that cool exterior slip.

'Dan?' Despite the smooth, polished exterior, slicked-back hair and shades, he saw the face of the man who'd once worn military fatigues alongside him.

'Giovanni?' His old mate grabbed him into a bear hug and slapped him heartily on the back.

'What on earth are you doing here?'

'Bodyguard for the spoiled teenager.' Dan grinned, letting Giovanni know exactly who his charge was.

'How did you get this gig?' Giovanni was curious for more than one reason.

'Same as you, probably. Did some work in security and earned myself a good reputation. Are you with Leanne's dance partner?'

'Yeah. Princess Francesca, but we need to keep it on the down low.' He was sure Dan would understand the need for discretion given they were in the same profession.

'No problem. Can't believe I'm seeing you here of all places.'

'I know. The last place I saw you—'

'Was in the hospital.' The smile on Dan's face died, and no wonder. It wasn't a happy time for either of them.

'You look well.' From the outside no one would ever have known he'd been involved in such a traumatic event, which had left him with life-changing injuries.

'I suppose you're wondering how I'm even standing.'

'No, I...yes.' There was no point in trying to be polite. The matter had been on his mind since the moment he'd spotted Dan.

Dan bent down and rapped on his lower right leg. 'Prosthetic. It took a while to get used to, but no one would even guess I had my leg blown off now.'

The casual mention of the explosion made Giovanni wince. The deafening roar, the ringing in his ears, and the dust and dirt raining down on him were all memories that were still raw for him. Not to mention the screams of his fellow squaddies. Now here he was, face to face with one of the men whose life had been changed for ever because of Giovanni's negligence.

'And it doesn't stop you from doing your job now?' Giovanni kept his eyes on the dancers, making sure that Francesca didn't suffer because of his incompetence too.

'No. It's easy. I've still got hands to shove any too eager fans or potential stalkers out of the way. You know as well as I do that this job is more about planning than physicality.'

'Don't I know it?' Giovanni grumbled, thinking about the mess he was currently in. Francesca was certainly taking her time finding out about her sister, and he hadn't seen any sign of Isabella in here so far.

'Have you seen any of the other guys from the unit?'

'No. I don't socialise much.' The truth was he'd been too ashamed of himself to stay in contact with the others when he'd walked away with just a few cuts and bruises. He didn't have the right to feel sorry for himself, yet his life had changed that day for ever too.

'Married?'

'No.'

'Most of us are now. Rossi and Dino both have kids, and I've got one on the way.'

Giovanni didn't know why that information surprised him. Probably because he'd kept himself shut off from the idea of sharing his life with anyone, and expected the others had done the same.

'Congratulations, Dan. I'm pleased for all of you.' He'd spent the better part of two decades imagining his old army friends miserable, all because of him, and it was difficult to process otherwise. It was the reason he'd shut himself off emotionally from those around him. Believing he didn't deserve a happy life when he'd stolen one from everyone else. Now it seemed as though he was running out of excuses to keep people at a distance.

'You know, it wasn't your fault, Giovanni.' As if reading his thoughts, Dan did his best to relieve him of that guilt once more.

'I should've been more aware of what was going on. It was my job to keep everyone safe.'

'You didn't mean for anyone to get hurt. You didn't plant the bomb. Stop blaming yourself for something that was beyond your control, bud.' Another slap on the back.

'A friend of mine said something similar.' He thought of Francesca trying to convince him of the same thing, and not wanting to accept it. Now it seemed as though he had no choice. Though neither Francesca, nor Dan, could convince him that his parents' crash wasn't his fault. He had form when it came to letting himself, and others, down. Even now he was abandoning his post to try and make amends for his old mistakes.

'Then maybe you should listen to her.' Dan followed Giovanni's gaze towards Francesca. If he was trying to insinuate there was something more going on than a job, he'd got it completely wrong. Even if Giovanni had inadvertently referred to her as a friend.

'It was good catching up with you, but I think it's time I got the Princess out of here before she's spotted.' He shook hands with Dan and headed back to the dance floor.

'Take care, Giovanni. And remember, none of it was your fault,' Dan called after him and the words rang in Giovanni's head even as he walked closer to the source of the deafening music.

'I think this is my cue to leave,' Francesca told Leanne, glad to see Giovanni arrive, as all her attempts to leave so far had been thwarted by a pouting pop star.

'Are you sure you can't stay?' Leanne was clinging to her hand.

'Sorry. I've got to find my sister, and if she's not here—' It had taken a while to establish that fact. Leanne had been sketchy about whether or not Isabella had been here, or even been in contact. Francesca suspected she just wanted a royal at her party, whoever that might be, and at whatever cost. In the end, frustrated, she'd had to ask directly. A sulky Leanne had reluctantly told her that she hadn't heard from Isabella since the wedding had been called off. So there was absolutely no reason for Francesca to stay. In fact, the longer she hung around, the greater the risk of her being snapped by someone.

'It's time to go.' Giovanni clearly heard the end of the conversation as he came back to join them, saving her once again.

'Thank you so much for a lovely time. Hopefully we'll meet again some time.' Francesca air-kissed Leanne on both cheeks before making a hasty exit from the club.

Thankfully, a well-known socialite was arriving just as Francesca and Giovanni were leaving. Someone only too happy to court the paparazzi, allowing the two reluctant partygoers to slip away virtually unnoticed.

They ran up the street, Giovanni's jacket covering their heads, laughing as they got one over on the press.

The moment of euphoria didn't last, however, when she remembered they'd hit another dead end.

'Now where do we go?' It was Giovanni who questioned their next move and it was unnerving to find he didn't know where they were going next either, when she'd become used to him taking the lead.

'Oh, Leanne said something about a street

party going on at South Bank. Maybe she went there?' In a city this size it was impossible to guess where one person might be, but she couldn't just sit in a hotel room doing nothing to try and find her sister.

Francesca had a duty to her family, and she always did her best to never let them down.

CHAPTER THREE

THEY MADE THEIR way over towards the South Bank. Against Giovanni's better judgement. At this stage he thought they'd be better off going back to the hotel to wait for Isabella to show up. This was like trying to find a needle in a haystack, and every moment Francesca was in public put her in potential danger. As well as giving the press plenty of photo opportunities if she was spotted. The only thing in her favour was that perhaps she wasn't as much of a well-known face in London as she was back home. If they stayed away from any more celebrity-filled parties, they might have a chance of keeping a low profile.

Even if he hadn't been her bodyguard, Giovanni would have felt protective over Francesca. He knew being out in the real world was a new experience for her and, despite her years, she was naïve. It came from a world of privilege where the family was protected from everything beyond the palace walls. She apparently hadn't known the dangers of simply walking around a city at night until she'd actually experienced it. Clutching on to him as though her life depended on it. No wonder she was so worried about her sister too.

Francesca's eyes were wide as she took in her surroundings. The throng of people, and the sights and smells of London at night. Any time they were in a crowded area, she moved a little closer to him. The bustling metropolis was alien to anyone who'd grown up on their small island, but Giovanni had plenty of experience, having travelled all over the world with the army. Perhaps this adventure would help Francesca broaden her horizons the way the army had for him. Then she'd realise that her position in the royal family wasn't the be-all and end-all for her. Even though it must feel like it at times.

They stopped along the side of the Thames so he could get his bearings, and the rumble of Francesca's stomach took them both by surprise.

'I'm so sorry.' Her cheeks pinked at the indelicate sound, but it was a reminder that she was human and needed sustenance like everyone else. It was easy for Giovanni to forget to eat on the job, and he grabbed food when he could, but someone like Francesca was used to scheduled, regular mealtimes, and her body wasn't going to let her forget.

'It's okay. You haven't had anything to eat since lunch. We can grab something here if you like?' He was aware that those fancy meals they served at official functions didn't equate to a proper meal anyway. A smear of sauce and a pretentiously placed asparagus tip on a blob of celeriac mash was not his idea of a good feed.

'Umm...' Francesca glanced apprehensively at the few log-cabin-style stalls dotted around selling street food. It dawned on him that she'd probably never eaten anything that wasn't presented by attentive silver service waiting staff.

Hers was a different world from the one he'd grown up in. Though he'd lost his parents when he was a teen, life before that had been relatively happy. They hadn't had a lot of money, and both his mother and father had worked hard to put dinner on the table. It meant he'd been at home alone a lot of the time, but he'd known he was loved. Sometimes he wondered if Francesca had that. Yes, she had everything money could buy, but he could tell she was lonely at times. He recognised it, having spent the best part of two decades keeping people at a distance. Francesca didn't seem to have a lot of people in her life that weren't required to be there because of her position. No real friends as far as he could see. No one to love her just for who she was.

'I'll order for us,' he said in the end, much to her apparent relief, and he opted for the 'dirty fries' option to satiate their hunger for now.

'What on earth is that?' Francesca prodded the congealed carbs in the cardboard box with her plastic fork. This was certainly a new experience for her.

'French fries loaded with cheese, fried onions and crispy bacon. I got you a beer too.'

They sat down at one of the bistro tables set out for customers and Giovanni watched her with fascination, waiting for a thumbs up, or down. She nibbled at first, and, once she worked up the courage, ventured to taste the liberal toppings. After the deliberation akin to a restaurant reviewer, she eventually went on to eat a second mouthful.

'It's not bad,' was the verdict. Though her face contorted when she took a slug of beer from the bottle, which apparently wasn't to her taste.

'I suppose you're more used to champagne.'

Giovanni regretted teasing her when he saw her flinch.

'It's not my fault.'

'I know. I was only joking.'

'You have no idea what it's like. It might seem like everybody's idea of heaven, but it's not like in the fairy tales. The wealth comes at a price you don't know about. Every move I make, everything I do, say, or wear, is calculated, because it's going to be picked apart. Whether it's by my parents, my peers, the press, or the general public, I'm always being scrutinised, and it's exhausting.'

'I understand there's a lot of pressure on you, Francesca, but you cope amazingly well.'

She flashed him a weak smile. 'That's what I want everyone to believe, because I'm a people pleaser. I have to be. I can't afford for anyone not to like me, can I? I'm going to be Queen one day. A position that depends very much on the country believing in me to do the job I was born for. Talk about pressure.'

Francesca knocked back the beer. Giovanni knew what it was like to want to drown those worries and fears in alcohol. He'd done his fair share of that over the years mourning for his parents, and after the bomb went off. It didn't achieve anything and he certainly wasn't going to offer to buy her another one.

'Everyone knows you can do it. I've never had a doubt.' Although she was a fish out of water here, she could certainly hold a room full of nobles and dignitaries. Francesca had a strong spirit. One he was sure was bursting to be free. Even for one night.

She raised an eyebrow. 'No? Not even tonight when I had no idea how to take a train, or had never eaten fast food?'

He shook his head. 'Different worlds, Princess. I'm sure I wouldn't know where to start addressing the nation, or what cutlery to use for eating peacock fritters.'

It took her a moment to realise he was making fun of her, but this time a grin spread across her lips. She lifted one of her fries and threw it at him, making him chuckle. 'Think of all the horror stories I'll have to tell my friends. That I actually ate food in the street, and had to use public bathrooms.'

Hands to her face, she gave him a mock scream, showing she was as game for a laugh as the next person. It was nice to see her this way, carefree, and like any other young woman her age. At least for the moment they were both able to forget she had the weight of a country's hopes and dreams on her shoulders. For the moment.

They smiled at one another, perhaps a fraction too long, something passing between them that went beyond their usual banter. If she weren't a princess, and Giovanni her bodyguard, he might've believed they were having the sort of moment most people longed for on a first date. The spark. That lingering eye contact denoting an interest in one another. The promise of spending more quality time together. Yet, in the circumstances, it could never be a possibility for them.

'We should probably get moving.' Unfortunately, they still had a mission to complete as quickly and discreetly as possible. He had to put all thoughts of Francesca, other than keeping her safe, out of his mind.

Giovanni grabbed their abandoned meals and bottles, throwing their rubbish into the relevant bins. 'The party's across the bridge. A quick look around and then we should probably call it a night.'

Francesca followed him over to the bridge, trying Isabella as she did so. 'Still no answer.'

'She might just be somewhere without a great reception. I'm sure she'll be in touch as soon as she can.' He was trying to convince them both of the best possible outcome.

'Isn't it beautiful?' Francesca marvelled as they joined the crowds streaming across the bridge.

It was lit up with blue neon, the city lights blazing around them. Apart from a few tourists taking pictures to post online, very few people seemed to notice the view, too focused on getting to their destination. That was something Giovanni had always admired about Francesca. Well, one of the many qualities in her he liked. She always took time to appreciate her surroundings, thanking her hosts, interacting with the public who came out to see her, accepting handmade cards and gifts as though they were the most precious things in the world to her.

Impromptu walkabouts in the crowds were a security nightmare but Francesca always took that time out from a busy schedule to acknowledge her surroundings, and the people who'd perhaps made a special trip to see her. It was no wonder she was popular with her subjects. Beautiful, smart, and caring—it was everything needed in a great monarch. The only blot on her otherwise perfect appearance was her disastrous love life.

He'd never thought Benigno worthy of her

love. He'd never seen any real evidence of it from Francesca either. It had frustrated him knowing she'd promised her life and future to a man who was no real match for her. Giovanni knew Francesca well enough to understand she needed someone with the same strength that she possessed. Someone who could support her when she became Queen and had to make difficult decisions.

That wasn't Benigno. He'd seemed a nice enough guy, but he was weak. As proved when he broke off the engagement. Although he was sorry for the scandal and heartbreak it had caused Francesca and her family at the time, it had been a relief to Giovanni. She deserved someone better. Someone she truly loved, because she was going to need them by her side when she had her struggles too.

Tonight was a good example. If she'd been doing this with Benigno goodness knew where she would've ended up, or what would've happened. At least Giovanni had her best interests at heart. Not just his own, or his family's prospects, the way Benigno had.

'We should take a picture to remember this moment,' Francesca told him as she leaned over the metal rails, breathing in the night air.

He produced his phone so he'd be the one

to have a record of it. With one arm around her, he held the camera up to capture the moment. Francesca placed a hand on his chest and kissed his cheek just as he snapped, the look of surprised joy on his face captured for ever. He quickly snapped another shot, this time making sure his usually impenetrable expression was on his face so he could show Francesca the photograph without fear of exposing his growing feelings towards her. The close call reminding him that the minute he let emotions get in the way of his job was the very moment she could end up getting hurt.

'Right. Let's get moving.' One thing was sure, standing here wasn't going to achieve anything.

When they reached the end of the bridge, they were transported into an altogether different atmosphere. Where the party in the club had been intense, there was much more of a carnival vibe with all the rides usually seen at a funfair, and stalls selling candyfloss and hot dogs.

'I wasn't expecting this.' Francesca clearly didn't know where to look first when there was so much going on.

'It's certainly not like any street party I've seen before.' He'd been very young when Francesca's father had come to the throne and they'd had a street party too. Except all he remembered was sitting at large trestle tables with jugs of orange squash and plates and plates of food and sweets. The only thing it had in common with this one was the bunting depicting the national flag of the respective countries, along with images of their new King. He'd even seen a few people wearing cardboard cut-out masks of the King. Which was disturbing to say the least.

'Isabella would love this. If she's going to be anywhere, it would be here.' Francesca's child-like wonder made him smile.

'I don't suppose you've been to anything like this before. My parents used to take me once a year to the fair at the harbour back home. I always remember those dark nights in October. The air smelled of bonfires and candyfloss. It was always cold, but I didn't care. I just wanted to have fun. The waltzers were my favourite.'

A smile played on his face at the memories he'd long forgotten. His parents waiting patiently as he jumped on ride after ride, never thinking about how much it cost, but knowing now they'd likely spent money they couldn't afford so that he could enjoy himself. It made his heart ache a little more for the family he'd once been a part of and had destroyed in one night of madness.

'We went once to a theme park, but they closed it to the public so that we wouldn't be bothered by anyone. It wasn't quite the same as this. I'd love to be a part of it all. Why don't we go on the waltzers now?' Francesca took his hand and walked him over to where a queue of people were standing waiting patiently for the previous riders to disembark.

'I'm not sure I'll enjoy it as much these days,' Giovanni protested too late as an excited Francesca pulled him into one of the cars and pulled the safety bar down.

Francesca was squeezing his hand, the adrenaline clearly pumping through her body. Once upon a time a fairground ride would have done the same for him, but he'd been in more adrenaline situations than this since. Why, then, did his pulse race every time she touched him?

'Here we go.' Francesca grabbed his arm and cuddled closer as they began to move. It was only natural to put his arm around her, to stop her from sliding up and down the seat as their car spun around. Her obvious joy doing more to his senses than the spinning around, music blaring, and lights flashing.

They got faster and faster, her shrieks coming louder in his ear. Then she let go of him, shot both arms in the air, closed her eyes, and gave herself over to the moment. As though she were completely free. It was a powerful moment to witness; to be part of. And his heart ached for her.

At least he'd had a taste of normality during his childhood. Francesca's had been a round of private tutors, etiquette lessons, and public engagements. With no more room to just be herself then, than as an adult. The least he could give her was a few hours to simply enjoy herself. Exactly the reason she and Isabella had sneaked out of their engagement in the first place.

When the ride stopped, after what had seemed like an eternity since the attendant had seen fit to give their car an extra swing every time he'd walked by, Giovanni helped Francesca out and back down to earth.

'Wow. I think my head's still spinning, and my legs are like jelly.' She laughed, clinging onto Giovanni for support.

'Yeah. I don't know why I ever thought that was fun.' Perhaps as he'd grown older his centre of gravity had changed, but he'd got more enjoyment out of watching Francesca's reaction than the actual ride itself.

'What are we going on next?' She spun around to face him, obviously addicted to the adrenaline rush already. He'd created a monster.

'Can we give it a few minutes? Er, we should probably have a look around for Isabella.' He didn't want her to think he needed time to recover before the next vomit-inducing whirligig.

'Yes. Of course.' The disappointment and shame were there in her expressive eyes. She looked torn between wanting to have fun and knowing she should be looking for her sister.

If there was one thing Giovanni knew about Francesca, it was that she always did the right thing. Especially where her family were concerned. Why else would she have got engaged to a man her family had deemed a suitable match, knowing she didn't love him?

'We can keep an eye out for her and take a wander around the stalls,' he suggested, doing his best to cover all bases and keep her happy.

It seemed to do the trick as she was soon smiling again.

'Ooh. I've seen these in the movies. I'd love to win one of those cuddly toys.' She spotted the hook-a-duck stall festooned with cheap plastic toys and impossible-to-win huge teddy bears. Still, he wouldn't deny her the chance to try. It might be the only time in her life she could.

Giovanni paid the man behind the lazy river of ducks floating by, and he handed Francesca a long pole with a hook on the end.

'I'll pay you back for all of this,' she promised. Both of them knowing it wasn't true. He doubted Francesca ever had any cash of her own. She'd never needed it since everyone around her took care of that sort of thing.

'It doesn't matter. Now, just catch one of the hooks on the ducks' heads on the way past.' Giovanni held the end of the pole to steady it, and let Francesca pick her duck. She deftly hooked it and lifted it up in triumph, as though she'd just caught a prize salmon.

'Got one!'

Her jubilation was short-lived as the attendant unhooked it and showed her the 'You Lose' scribbled on the bottom in black marker.

'Don't worry. We can try somewhere else.' Seeing her disappointment, Giovanni went against his better judgement and moved to a target shoot a few stalls along.

All he had to do was shoot a ball bearing into a winning playing card. A piece of cake for the ex-soldier. Except he'd forgotten these places were always rigged to dupe the unsuspecting public.

'The sights are off,' he growled to the teen manning the booth.

The boy shrugged. 'I just work here, mate.'

Francesca grew restless beside him, and he knew he had to prove himself. Male bravado took over, and he took aim again with a new determination. He made adjustments this time for the wonky sights and fired the shot bang in the centre of the target.

Francesca squealed and fuelled him on to make the same shot two more times.

'Take your pick,' the unimpressed attendant told him, pointing to the cuddly toys hung around the booth.

'You heard him, take your pick.' Giovanni was pumped with pride, like a teenager on a date showing off for his girl.

'I guess you never lose it, huh?' She nudged him with her hip before taking her time selecting her prize.

'Something like that.' It wasn't quite the same as being on the shooting range, or providing cover fire for an army colleague, but he'd still got a buzz out of displaying his prowess.

'Can I have that one, please?' Francesca selected a huge pink teddy bear wearing a tiara.

'Very apt.'

'Thank you so much. This is like a dream come true. Except, you know, without the missing-sister and trying-to-dodge-the-press parts.' Then she did something completely unexpected by standing up on her tiptoes and kissing him on the cheek.

Such a public display of affection not only completely against her usual protocol, but also showing him that perhaps he had become more to her than a constant shadow reminding her that she was never alone.

A wake-up call for him to keep his thoughts on the job.

Francesca was practically floating on air. This night had become more than she could ever have dreamed. The only dark spot being the spectre of Isabella's disappearance. She felt guilty about enjoying herself but had to console herself with the thought that her sister was probably out there having a whale of a time with someone too. If she didn't believe that she'd never manage to keep it together.

Strolling around the fair with her giant teddy bear under one arm, and Giovanni's hand in hers, she'd never been so content. Relaxed. Free. He was being so accommodating, and, though he was always attentive to her security needs, tonight he seemed to be paying her personal attention. Something had bonded them tonight and she didn't know if it was the mutual feeling of jeopardy as they'd gone in search of Isabella or opening up to one another a little about their lives that had done it. She just knew their relationship was never going to be the same again.

The kiss on the cheek had been spontaneous, but had felt natural in the circumstances. It wasn't as though she'd snogged his face off, but the effect on her had been just the same. She couldn't get it out of her mind. The feel of his stubble rasping against her lips, the smell of his so familiar aftershave, and the look on his face were all things she'd never forget. Especially when he hadn't seemed to mind. There had been no stern scowl, or admonishment, but a fleeting expression of...interest?

She couldn't help but let her imagination run away and wonder what it would feel like to kiss him. A thought she'd had many times before. It was impossible not to when he was so handsome, and a constant presence in her life. But now she had some reality to add to the fantasy. What if he'd enjoyed it too? What if he'd kissed her back with the passion she was sure lingered there behind the cool exterior? Especially when she'd had glimpses of the real Giovanni tonight, and the very real emotions, which weren't as far beneath his surface as he liked to portray.

Not that she could do anything about it anyway. Even if they both liked each other, there was no way her parents would approve of the match. She would have to be with someone of noble birth to gain their approval and she couldn't risk losing their support simply because she fancied her bodyguard. Any desire she felt towards him, that longing for a normal relationship, would have to remain a fantasy for ever. If she let herself go, she was worried this poised princess would completely unravel, and never get back to who she was supposed to be.

'How do you feel about heights?' he asked, out of the blue.

'I have no problem. Why?' She'd spent a lifetime flying in helicopters and jets, and had had no option but to become accustomed to it. The royal family would never usually be allowed to take public transport. It was too great a security risk if nothing else.

He turned his gaze to the Ferris wheel looming over the whole fairground. 'It means we can sit down for a while, but will also give us a good view in case Isabella is nearby.'

'Good thinking.' If nothing else she could take her shoes off for a while.

As had happened so often on this night out, Francesca could only stand and watch as Giovanni paid their fare. It was such a little, but necessary, thing to carry cash or a credit card, which hadn't occurred to her or Isabella at all. An important reminder, not only of how much they took for granted, but also of how removed they were from the rest of the world. It was a lesson she was going to take back with her. When she did eventually become Queen, she knew the memories she was making tonight were going to help her relate better to the people she would rule over.

They waited on the short platform for their car to come around and quickly stepped in, practically falling onto the long seat as they swung back and forth. Her big teddy bear had ended up wedged between them and part of her was missing that closeness she'd enjoyed with Giovanni most of the night.

'You can see for miles.' As they were lifted up into the air, the people below them grew smaller and smaller, but there was still no sign of Isabella. She had hoped that her sister's blazing-red dress might've been easy to spot from this position, but perhaps she hadn't come here at all.

'We can try somewhere else.' Giovanni seemed to know exactly what to say every time her heart sank.

Francesca sat back in her seat, realising she'd been leaning out a tad too far for her liking, in her attempt to locate Isabella.

'I wish she would just let me know that she's okay so I could stop worrying. Typical Isabella. As the youngest she thinks she can do whatever she pleases without fear of reprisals. I suppose she's right.'

Giovanni laughed. 'I thought you were twins.'

'We are, but that whole five minutes between us makes all the difference. We might have done everything together growing up, been taught the same values, and shown how we were supposed to act. In the end, though, there's only one of us who'll have to give up her life to rule the country.'

She knew she sounded bitter, but it was cathartic to get that off her chest. There was no one else she could voice that frustration to. The injustice of that five minutes controlling her whole existence was something she'd held inside her for too long. There was nothing

Giovanni, or anyone else, could do about it, but for once she'd felt able to say exactly what she thought. Even if it had left her trembling.

'Is that why you were going to marry Benigno? Because it was expected of you?'

She was stunned by his insight, but she supposed he'd been with her long enough to have realised she hadn't been with her ex because it was a love match. 'He was deemed acceptable to marry a future queen. Who was I to argue?'

She'd liked Benigno, tried to make the relationship work, and thought she'd been the perfect fiancée, attentive and supportive—she'd done everything she could to please him. In the end it hadn't been sufficient to keep them together. Just like her relationship with her parents, simply being her wasn't enough.

Perhaps it had been lacking an emotional commitment on her part. Something that was going to mar any partnership when she'd been taught to lock that part of herself away. Devoting everything to her position, and her future, instead of giving her heart any say in what happened to her. A sign of weakness. In future she was going to have to consider a marriage of convenience to someone who was more interested in status than love. Preferably to a man who understood the pressures on her, and that her loyalty was to the crown and country, not her personal life. The perfect royal, if not the perfect wife.

She was the one who should be scowling at the thought of her fate, not Giovanni.

'It's your life, Francesca. You should get a say in it. Especially when it comes to marriage. When you are Queen, you're going to need someone who can support you, who you can turn to, who you love. Sorry, it's not my place to say anything on such matters.'

Giovanni's passionate expression of his feelings on the matter only made her shiver more. She hadn't realised he even had an opinion, never mind that he cared what happened to her when it came to marriage. He wasn't just a big wall of stone after all.

Giovanni moved her bear out of the way and took his jacket off to put it around her again. 'Here, you're freezing.'

Francesca didn't tell him it wasn't the cold making her quiver, but the chance to finally vent. 'I'm so sorry I didn't have the forethought to wear an outer layer. We can share. It's going to get colder the further up we go.'

'I suppose you're just used to temperature-controlled venues. Not too hot, not too cold, just like Goldilocks.' Giovanni didn't protest as she rearranged his jacket to sit around both of their shoulders, drawing them closer together.

If this had been a date, it would've been perfect. It made her wonder if they weren't who they were to her family, and the rest of the world, would he have taken her out and treated her like this? She wanted the answer to be yes, but at the same time it made her sad that she'd never get to experience this again. Certainly not with a bodyguard who took his job extremely seriously. This was simply a very nice anomaly she should savour for what it was.

'I know, I know. I've been spoiled. I do realise there are people working very hard behind the scenes to make things happen around me and it's not down to little woodland creatures catering to my every whim.' If it hadn't been for Giovanni tonight she would've been completely lost. And she and Isabella had thought they could just run around London... Francesca liked to think she wasn't as naïve as she had been a couple of hours ago.

'I think you're one of the few people who does show her appreciation. I've been around my share of supermodels and movie stars—'

'Oh?' Francesca couldn't stop the wave of jealousy welling up and spilling out of her mouth.

'Work related. I did have a life before you,

you know. Anyway, I've seen truly spoiled
and it's not you. Privileged, yes, but I don't believe you take people for granted and that's the
main thing. It's what will make you an excel-
lent queen.' Giovanni's sincerity, along with the
nice things he was saying, made her well up.

Perhaps she wasn't as awful as she sometimes thought, when nothing she did seemed
to make her parents happy. They were always
correcting her, telling her how she should have
done things, so she never knew if she was
doing a good job or not. It wasn't as though
members of the royal family got an 'employee
of the month' award so they knew they were
on the right track. Perhaps that was something
she could look to implement in the future. With
extra stars awarded to anyone who managed
to stay out of the gossip columns on a regular
basis. Something that would be a miracle if she
and Isabella managed to achieve it.

First picture on the wall would be Giovanni's
for guiding her through this mess. And saying
nice things she really needed to hear.

'Thank you.' As they reached the top of the
ride, it slowed down to let people off. Up here,
the noise of the fairground seemed far away.
The city lights spread before them like a carpet of brightly coloured stars.

Francesca leaned her head on Giovanni's shoulder with a sigh, knowing this moment of peace wouldn't last for ever. He didn't move away from her, instead pulled her closer so that she could share his body heat and enjoy the safe reassurance of his solid body beneath her.

When the wheel began to move again her mood changed to one of despair. She knew the closer they got to the ground, the sooner she would have to face reality.

Eventually she had no choice but to grab her teddy bear and jump off onto the platform. Francesca checked her phone again. Tried calling Isabella, and left another message.

'What do you want to do now?' Giovanni stood beside her waiting for instruction, apparently having run out of ideas too.

Francesca checked her watch. 'It's getting late. Places will be closing soon.'

'Not the clubs. They'll be open to all hours. It's not like back home. You can party all night in London.' Giovanni was so much more a man of the world, but even he didn't have sister-seeking superpowers to help them find Isabella.

'I'm all out of ideas. We're just on a wild goose chase. And as much as I've enjoyed having these new experiences with you, I'm worried about being spotted. If Isabella comes back like nothing happened, and I'm the one who makes the papers, it'll be me our parents will be mad at. Or, worse, they'll tell me how disappointed in me they are.'

She couldn't win. In the end she'd be the one to bear the brunt of blame if any of this came out. For not keeping Isabella in line, for running loose around London, and for bringing the family name into disrepute. As future Queen, she was the one who should've known better. Even if she didn't regret the time she'd got to spend with Giovanni away from the social restraints they usually had to abide by.

'It's a lot of responsibility on your shoulders. I know how difficult it is to live with that burden, but I also know you've done your best. Always. We need to keep you safe too, Francesca. However, I do think I need to alert the rest of the security team that Isabella is missing. I wouldn't be doing my job otherwise.'

He gently broached the subject she'd been trying to avoid, because once the news was out there that Isabella was missing in London, it was going to become a worldwide story. One that no one was going to thank her for. Including her sister if she had gone off on her own accord.

'Can we check back at the hotel first to see if she's there? If not, I promise we'll make things official.' Francesca had to concede defeat. They'd tried their best to track Isabella down, but it was clear she didn't want to be found. Either that or she was enjoying herself so much she hadn't given a thought to anyone who might be missing her.

Francesca prayed for the latter, though it didn't mean she wouldn't read her sister the Riot Act when they did eventually locate her.

'Okay, but if we don't see or hear from her then I'm going to have to call it in.' Though Giovanni wasn't happy, Francesca was glad he was willing to give her more time to track down Isabella.

She understood that this situation was a nightmare for him too because he hadn't stopped them from going off in the first place. They'd appreciated his discretion at the time, but she realised now the price it had cost him. If anything happened to Isabella, Giovanni would feel to blame every bit as much as she would. Another casualty of their selfish decision-making. They hadn't taken anyone else's feelings into account tonight in pursuit of their own good time. In future she would do everything Giovanni advised when he knew best.

Straight after she enjoyed her last moments of freedom.

'There's just one stop I'd like to make on the way back, if that's okay?'

CHAPTER FOUR

AGAINST HIS BETTER JUDGEMENT—which had happened a lot tonight—Giovanni agreed to make one last pitstop before he got Francesca safely back to the hotel. He had hoped that once she was asleep he might be able to track down Isabella himself, with instruction to hotel security not to let the Princess leave her room under any circumstances. It was touch and go whether they'd still get out of this mess unscathed.

By letting her have her way now he thought he might have a chance at getting her to comply for the rest of the evening.

It was the choice of venue that had him scratching his head.

'Why Westminster Abbey?' He would've thought it was the last place she'd want to be. It was where they'd spent the better part of the day waiting and watching the King's coronation. The symbol of everything she seemed to be dreading.

'Just humour me.' She stood across from the building, staring at the Gothic architecture of the abbey, lit up in the darkness. As though picturing her own coronation day.

'It's not going to do you any good fretting over things you have no control over.' He did his best to get her to leave instead of torturing herself even more when she already had Isabella's disappearance to worry about.

'Uh-huh? Like you blaming yourself for a bomb that someone else planted?' Arms folded, chin tilted up in defiance, she fired his own issues back at him.

Giovanni exhaled slowly. 'We've been over this. It was my fault we were there. My fault I didn't realise the danger ahead.'

'Do you think that they blame you? That they want you to spend the rest of your life feeling sorry for yourself?' This was the Francesca he knew. The fiery one he got to see beyond the cool façade, who wasn't afraid to call anyone out on their nonsense. A true version he'd like to see take the throne, free from the constraints her parents put on her.

Though in this case, someone else had already made him face this particular demon head-on.

'No.' Finally admitting it was like taking a deep, cleansing breath. Regardless that he still had another black spectre haunting his soul.

Nothing could change the fact that he'd lost the only family he'd had. The only family he was likely to ever have. No matter how much he yearned to have that cosy domestic scene in his life again, he couldn't risk a partner, or a child, getting hurt on account of him. So he'd lived a solitary existence. Kept relationships brief and non-committal. Regardless of how lonely he was at times. He couldn't run the risk of causing more loved ones pain. Nor could he face losing anyone else.

Moving on from his guilt didn't mean he was free to gamble with people's lives, or his own heart.

Francesca blinked those big whisky-coloured eyes at him. She clearly hadn't expected him to agree so readily. It seemed only fair to explain his change of heart. Then perhaps she might start to see that holding onto that kind of baggage was detrimental.

'I ran into one of them back at the club. Dan. He's doing security for that Leanne person now.'

'But I thought they'd all been seriously injured?'

'They were. He was. He lost part of his leg, but he's wearing a prosthetic. Apparently, they're all doing well. Happy. Adjusted. Settled.' It was everything he could've hoped for for his old army buddies, but he couldn't help but envy them too. All things he would never be.

'So now you can let go? It's time you got on with your life.'

'It's not that easy, Francesca.'

'Why not? They've moved on. They're still alive—'

'But my parents *aren't*.' He hadn't meant to be sharp with her, but the guilt and pain were never far from the surface.

The questioning look from Francesca was understandable since she knew nothing about his background, and why should she when he was supposed to just be the hired help?

'Anyway, that's my problem. You wanted to come here so we should probably go and let you have a last look at the abbey.' He made a move to walk over but Francesca remained steadfast.

'I thought we were way beyond keeping a professional distance, Giovanni. You know more about me than anyone. Including my own family. Please let me in.' The plea went straight to his heart. The very place he didn't want to unlock. For Francesca's sake as much as his own.

He shook his head. 'Everyone that gets close to me ends up hurt. I can't risk being with anyone. My job is my life.'

She gave a bitter laugh. 'Same.' Then she cocked her head. 'Though for different reasons, I suspect. Apparently, I'm cold and unemotional. All the things I've been brought up to be, so I stay in line.'

'Francesca, I know you are neither of those things.' Tonight was just one example. If she didn't love her sister so much she wouldn't have gone ahead with tonight, never mind being out of her head with worry now about Isabella's safety. He'd been to enough functions and public appearances to know that the way she interacted with and cared for people went against any idea of her being cold and emotionally distant. If that had come from Benigno, there was a good reason for that. Because she'd never loved him, and she'd admitted as much herself.

'I didn't mean to hurt Benigno. I thought he knew about the arrangement between our families and what he was getting himself into.

I tried to make it work but I guess I wasn't enough. I probably never will be for any man, when I can't give anyone the attention they apparently need. My duty will always have to come first.'

'I suspect it wasn't so much naïvety on his part, but a damaged ego that you didn't turn into a simpering fool for him. He's probably used to being top dog, and he could never hope to compete with the standing of a future queen. A real man wouldn't need to.' If someone truly loved Francesca and had her best interests at heart he'd never ask, or expect, her to prioritise him over her country.

'It doesn't matter now, does it?' She shrugged. 'Anyway, stop changing the subject. Tell me about your parents since you seem determined to let whatever happened steal a life away from the palace from you.'

Since they were going to be together for some time yet tonight, he knew she wasn't going to let the matter drop. It was of no consequence when nothing she said could possibly change what happened, or how he felt about it.

'I was eighteen. Used to doing what I wanted because my parents were always out working. I got drunk one night, made a nuisance of myself around town and got picked up by the police. It wasn't anything serious and they knew my parents, so they called home and asked my dad to come and pick me up.' It still hurt to think about, knowing he'd got them both out of bed, and they'd still been wearing their pyjamas when their bodies had been recovered.

'Okay…doesn't sound too terrible. Lots of people do stupid things when it comes to alcohol.' Despite her attempt to placate him, Giovanni knew Francesca had never had the luxury of misbehaving in such a manner. As far as he was aware she'd never put a foot out of line. Until tonight.

'They were hit by a truck. It was never clear who was in the wrong. It's possible my dad was still half asleep at that time of the morning. They were both killed on impact.' Not that hearing that had ever been any consolation. If it hadn't been for him, they'd have still been in their beds sleeping soundly.

'I'm so sorry, Giovanni. That must've been so awful for you. You've been through so much.' The pity in her eyes for him was too much to look at. He didn't deserve it.

'More like I've been the cause of it. Now you know. I'm cursed. So are those closest to me.'

'And so you've lived a lonely life, to spare anyone else being hurt… I understand the

logic. Sort of. But it's the workings of a grief-
stricken teenager's mind. You know you
weren't to blame for that truck hitting your parents, any more than you were for the bomb that
was planted. Besides which, your army mates
want you to move on and I'm sure your parents would want you to do so too. It's not fair
on you to keep holding onto this guilt. You're
not going to gain anything from it, other than
being a martyr to yourself.'

Francesca was the first person he'd ever
opened up to about the guilt he felt over his
parents' deaths. He didn't even know why he
was doing so after all this time of knowing
her. Likely because tonight had been all about
firsts and breaking the rules.

He knew she wasn't the sort of person to
just tell him to pull himself together and get
over it, even if 'your parents wouldn't want
this' amounted to the same thing. Francesca
wanted him to think about the sacrifice he'd
made, giving up a life of his own as atone-
ment for his loved ones being hurt. Yet nothing was ever going to bring them back. All he
was doing was denying himself a chance to be
happy. Seeing Dan, hearing about the lives he
and the others had made for themselves had
made him see that. He just wasn't sure if his

fear of cursing those close to him would prevent him from moving on completely.

Loving someone meant the possibility of losing them and getting hurt all over again. Giovanni had already lost too much to go through that again. Even if the curse wasn't real, the devastation of people leaving him was, and that wasn't something he could easily forget. Even Francesca was going to get married some day and move on, and who knew if he would still be a part of her life at all?

'And what about you, Princess? Aren't you being a martyr by giving up any idea of love to please your parents?' If they were going to have a therapy session, it was about time someone tried to make Francesca see sense too. She deserved to have love in her life.

Her lips were a thin line of disapproval as he clawed back a point in their game of do as I say, not as I do. 'It's different for me. I have a duty to the whole country.'

'As a future queen, yes. As a woman, you're still entitled to have a personal life. Something just for you.'

'I wish it was as easy as that. I'm afraid tonight is all I have. You know I can't have a normal life. That's what this whole escapade was about. Giving me one night of freedom.

Pretending I don't have the weight of an entire country depending on me. There's no room for anyone else.'

'I don't believe that. I think you're just afraid of being vulnerable if you let yourself be open to the idea of loving someone. Risking that rejection and loss you felt from Benigno when things didn't work out.' It was easy to see the flaws in her logic, because deep down they were his too. Seeing them reflected in someone he cared about was beginning to make him see how self-destructive those wrongful, long-held beliefs could be.

Francesca opened and closed her mouth, a witty comeback not forthcoming, because she knew he was right. She'd spent her whole life making sure she lived up to people's expectations. She couldn't bear to let anyone down. Not her parents, her sister, her subjects, or a future husband. At least with an arranged marriage she wouldn't be so emotionally invested in making it work. The thought of loving someone, of letting down those barriers she'd built around her heart, terrified her. It had been drilled into her to be stoic at all times. Never show weakness. To her, that was exactly what loving someone represented. Why else would her parents have kept her at an emotional distance for her entire life?

'Do you know why I wanted to come back here, Giovanni? To remind me of the role model I'm supposed to be. One day I'm going to be the one who wears the crown. I've been in danger of forgetting that sometimes tonight.' She gave him a rueful smile. That wasn't entirely a bad thing. It was exactly why Isabella had suggested this in the first place.

Though that freedom had also made her forget why she shouldn't allow herself to be tempted by Giovanni. At times it had been easy to get caught up in the fantasy of being with him for real. Letting her feelings towards him run unchecked so she could imagine he was her partner, not her bodyguard. Unfortunately, he wasn't.

However, the longer she was away from her parents' influence, and her responsibilities, the weaker her defences were becoming. Until she almost felt normal. A dangerous position for someone of her status to find herself in. As if anything was possible. Now here was Giovanni trying to convince her of the same. That even love could be within her reach.

'I don't think the monarchy is going to crumble because you had a night off being Prin-

cess. Though you're always a princess to me.'
Giovanni reached into his jacket pocket and
pulled out the plastic tiara they'd been given
at the club. He placed it on top of her head and
arranged her hair around it.

She held her breath as he touched her, watching him carefully until he caught her staring.
He held her gaze, and if this had been a movie,
it would have been the moment he leant in for
a kiss, unable to resist her. Unfortunately, he
managed to control himself, and Francesca was
forced to get a hold on her own feelings too.

'I think it looked better on you,' she teased,
recalling the unamused look on his face at the
time, with joy. Doing her best to put the moment behind them and forget the hungry way
he'd looked at her.

She resisted placing the tiara back on his
head to replay the moment in the club, fear-
ful that if she touched him she would forget
herself entirely. This feeling of wanting something forbidden scared her. Never having been
so tempted to step out of her 'good girl' shoes.
The very reason she needed to avoid any more
lingering touches and longing glances.

There were many memories of tonight she
would keep with her for ever. Even if she
never got to do anything like this again, noth-

ing could take away this time she'd had with Giovanni. Getting to know him, really talking about things that mattered to her, and actually having fun. All in public and, hopefully, without her true identity being uncovered.

'I do wonder when my big day will happen. How I will feel. If my father will be alive to see it.' Given his health, he might not make it and the thought terrified her, of losing not only a parent, but a mentor. No one could coach her through life as a monarch as her father could. She knew there was talk of him abdicating. His cancer diagnosis and the ensuing complications had made him think about his own mortality. He wasn't an old man by any means and in order to prolong his life both of her parents thought he should slow down. Perhaps step back altogether. Though that would be a preferable scenario to him dying, Francesca didn't know if she was ready to take his place.

'All things which you have no control over,' he reminded her.

'It doesn't stop my mind constantly thinking about it all. Replaying today, only with me as the star of the show. Feeling the weight of that crown, heavy on my very soul.'

'You sound as though you don't really want the position.'

Francesca realised she'd said too much, but she trusted Giovanni. In fact, she was beginning to think he was the only person she could really talk to. 'It's not as though I have a choice.'

'It mightn't seem like it, but you could refuse to take the crown. The question is, do you really want to be Queen?'

It was a question no one had ever asked her before. As though she didn't have any say in the matter at all. Only Giovanni seemed to realise she was a real person who might have thoughts and needs of her own. It was something she had to think about. Being a normal person was tempting, but she couldn't shake off her responsibilities, even theoretically. Her parents would never forgive her. Perhaps some sort of concession might make the position more enjoyable, but she'd have to be strong enough to ask for it.

'Yes. It's the role I've been prepping for my whole life. It's just that it comes with great expectations and responsibilities, and that's a lot of pressure. There's no room for error.'

'You're only human, Francesca.'

'Tell that to my parents,' she said, unguarded. Though it wouldn't come as a surprise to

Giovanni to know the demands they put upon her when he was a constant by her side.

'Maybe you should.' Giovanni didn't look as if he was joking. In fact, by the set of his jaw he was deadly serious.

'Pardon?'

'Tell them how you feel. It's going to be a difficult enough job without trying to win their approval at the same time.'

Francesca felt seen, really seen, for the first time. As though he'd looked deep into her soul and plucked out her innermost fear. Disappointing her parents.

'It's not as easy as that…' she mumbled, caught off guard by his insight.

'Why not? When you're Queen you can do as you please. I'd say asking to have more control in your life is one of the smaller decisions you'll have to make.' He gave her a half-smile that contrasted with the huge grenade he'd just tossed in her direction.

As unbelievable as it seemed, she'd never imagined simply asking her parents to back off and give her more say in her own life, knowing it would upset them if she challenged them at all.

Perhaps if she actually did that, stood up and took control, her parents would be more inclined to trust her judgement on the big decisions she knew were coming.

'You should look into becoming a royal advisor instead of a royal protection officer.' If she'd had this conversation with him a long time ago, had Giovanni's support, she might've found the courage to forge her own path sooner.

Giovanni's deep laugh warmed her insides. 'I think I'll stick to the day job, thanks.'

'Yes, royal matters are not for the faint-hearted,' Francesca said with a sigh, realising with Giovanni's help, and despite feeling otherwise at times, she was made of strong stuff. She'd simply let herself be cowed by her parents, and, desperate to win their approval, had let their voices drown out her own. Something she would need to get a grip of before she did become Queen, when she wanted to be the strongest royal she could be. For her sake as well as that of the country.

'Yet this is the place you wanted to visit.' Giovanni gestured towards Westminster Abbey, which had been full of pomp and ceremony only hours ago. Everything she'd just told him she was worried about being a part of. 'Again, the word martyr comes to mind.'

Francesca stuck out her tongue. 'That's not why I wanted to come. I thought I needed some grounding after our time at the fair. It's the most fun I've ever had in my life.'

'Now that is a sad story,' Giovanni teased.

She nudged him in the ribs with her elbow. 'You know what I mean. Sitting at the top of that wheel was the freest I've ever been. It's tempting to never go back and live here in anonymity.'

It had also been one of her happiest memories. Just sitting with Giovanni, pressed close to his warmth, the world a million miles below them. In her dreams she'd be going home with him tonight, staying here for ever, having a normal life.

'You could never live in the shadows, Francesca. You will always shine.' The way Giovanni was looking at her made her heart leap. As though they were simply a man and a woman, with no gulf between them. Never more so than when he leaned into her and she felt the soft touch of his lips on hers.

Kissing Giovanni was something she'd daydreamed about, and the reality was more than she could ever have imagined.

If he expected her to push him away in disgust, stunned into silence by his audacity, he was very much mistaken. Whatever the reason for the kiss, she wasn't going to be the one to end it. Instead, she wrapped her arms around his neck and sought his tongue with hers, deepening the connection. She was sure she felt the reverberation of a growl against her lips, as he pulled her closer, his hands at her waist. If she could have this on tap, ready to go every time she worried about something, she'd be a very happy woman.

His lips were soft, yet demanding, and he tasted of beer and all things forbidden. He was addictive and she couldn't get enough. The teddy bear abandoned in the heat of their passion. A connection that was surprising, but, oh, so enjoyable. They'd always been close, even if they'd butted heads at times, but even in her fevered dreams she'd never imagined he would kiss her with such hunger. As though he'd been waiting for this moment as long as she had.

Unfortunately, Giovanni finally made the decision to end it. He pulled away, and took a step back.

'I'm sorry, Your Highness. I had no right to do that.'

'What if I wanted you to?' Francesca tried to close the distance between them, reaching for him, but he backed away.

'It doesn't matter. I shouldn't have done it. I overstepped. Please forgive me.'

'There's nothing to forgive you for, Giovanni.' She didn't know how else to make him realise she wanted to kiss him. Again, if possible.

'I just wanted to stop you from worrying, and now I've given us both an extra problem to deal with.'

'It doesn't have to be a problem if we don't make it one. A kiss can just be a kiss.' A million kisses could just be a million kisses and send her to bed with a smile on her face.

'Don't, Francesca. We both know I've messed up.'

'I'm not going to let you take the blame for this as well, Giovanni. Yes, you kissed me, but, let's face it, I was a willing partner.' She didn't want him to add to his burden of guilt when that kiss had been something she'd fantasised about for a lifetime. His guilt and regret would only tarnish the memory she was going to hold close to her heart for some time to come.

'Just…just check in on your sister again. I need to clear my head.' Giovanni turned away from her and began pacing, his hands on his head as though he'd just committed the crime of the century and didn't know how to handle it. Instead of this simply being two people drawn to one another because of their emotional wounds, and it having nothing to do with him being paid to be there.

She walked over to the abbey, determined to walk those steps the King had walked this morning. Facing his subjects, and a life devoted to them. Knowing his future was mapped out for ever, with no escape from his duty. She just hoped she showed as much courage as he had today when the time came.

'It looks as though someone had a little party here of their own after hours.' Giovanni walked over swinging a pair of red heels on the end of his finger.

Francesca took a cursory glance, her attention caught up in her own thoughts. Then she took a second look and snatched the shoes from Giovanni.

'These are Isabella's. Where did you find them? What exact position did you find them in?' All thoughts disappeared but those concerning the safety of her sister.

'They were just lying on the steps like she'd kicked them off. Maybe her feet were sore, like yours. She didn't have a bodyguard in shiny loafers to customise them for her.' Giovanni was attempting to lift the mood, but all that was coursing through Francesca's veins was pure panic. All the time she was living it up, fantasising she was on a date with her hot bodyguard, her sister could've been in real trouble. Exactly why frivolous emotions like desire were to be avoided. She couldn't afford to be so easily distracted from the important stuff going on around her.

'Or maybe they fell off when she was abducted. If someone grabbed her from behind she might have lost them in the struggle. She might even have left them here for me as a clue.' Francesca knew she was spiralling but guilt was overwhelming her that she hadn't taken Isabella's disappearance more seriously.

Giovanni cupped her face in his hands, making her look at him, just as he had in the club. 'We don't know that. She might have just gone barefoot. We both know your sister's a bohemian at heart.'

Francesca wanted to believe his smile and words of reassurance, but her in-built anxiety wouldn't let her. 'I should have let you call the police. If anything happens to her it'll be my fault—'

Francesca didn't know what to do other than give into the urge to cry, so she followed his instruction to try and check in with her sister again. Taking her phone from her bag with shaking hands, she saw that she had missed a voice message, and her racing pulse seemed to come to an abrupt halt.

'Giovanni? Isabella has left me a message. How could I have missed it?' Her one chance to speak to her sister, to find out where she'd gone, or if she was okay, and Francesca had been too busy snogging her bodyguard to notice.

'It probably came through when we were on the Tube. You don't get great reception down there.' Giovanni came back in a couple of strides, keen to hear the message for himself.

He stood close to her so they could both hear it when she pressed play.

'I'm so sorry, but I'm okay. I'll be back soon.' That was it. That was the message.

Francesca could feel her blood starting to boil. 'It's nearly midnight. We've spent most of the night chasing after her, not knowing if she's alive or dead, and that's all she could give me. "I'm okay. I'll be back soon."' She clicked her tongue against her teeth, really wanting to throw something, or scream. Preferably at her inconsiderate sister.

'Well, at least you know she's alive. And safe.' Giovanni had dropped his tortured soul act and gone back to being her jovial travelling companion.

As though nothing had happened. Francesca didn't know who was aggravating her more. In the end she unleashed her frustration on the expensive shoes in her line of sight. Picking them up and lobbing them one by one into the dark with a yell.

'Do you feel better for that?'

'Yes.' No.

'I'm sure the unsuspecting late-night passer-by you probably hit on the head with a flying stiletto is glad.'

'There's no one else around.' She wasn't going to let him guilt-trip her about finally letting go of some of her frustration. There was more than enough of that to go around.

'Would you like me to go and look for your sister's shoes?' He couldn't keep the amusement from his voice, but if he thought this was going to distract her from what had just happened between them, he was mistaken.

'No. She has plenty of shoes. Including the emergency ones she keeps in her bag, which I'd forgotten about. All she had to do was tell me where she was, Giovanni. Then we could have gone and got her. Crisis over. She couldn't even give me that.' Francesca was exhausted. Her emotions had been on a ride of their own to-night, between everything she felt for Giovanni and the worry over her sister. Isabella must've known she was going out of her mind with worry, but still she couldn't put her sister's feelings above her own for once.

'She's not your responsibility, Francesca. She's mine.' He went and retrieved the shoes.

'You don't get it, do you?' she shouted after him. 'Everyone…everything…it's all my responsibility. Sooner or later I'm going to be Queen, and whatever Isabella gets up to will come back on me.'

'You have to let her make her own decisions. Her own mistakes. You have to trust her.'

'And what do I do in the meantime? Just wait, biting my nails until she decides to show up?'

'Yes. Well, apart from the nails thing. I'm sure that manicure was expensive.' He was on fire with the jokes tonight, in between the heart-to-hearts and the kissing. She supposed it was to deflect the emotional vulnerability he'd shown tonight.

'Why do I have to be the sensible one? Always doing the right thing. Five minutes is all that stands between us, and yet it's a world of difference. Well, maybe I'm sick of it. Maybe I want to do whatever I want for one night too.

Answerable to no one. Just acting on pure impulse.'

The fire inside her was burning bright, the injustice of her position getting the better of her for once. Usually, she was able to temper it down, but tonight had been about being honest, and emotionally available. That was the problem, and why she didn't usually even entertain the idea. But it was too late tonight. That door had been left open and she couldn't stuff her feelings back inside just yet.

So she did what she'd wanted to do for a very long time, and kissed Giovanni.

Giovanni knew he should resist, and he did at first, but he was only human. And the fact that Francesca was taking such a risk to kiss him in public said that she hadn't been able to fight this chemistry either. He'd made a mistake in kissing her, telling himself it was the only way to stop her freaking out. When in fact it was all he'd been able to think about doing for most of the night.

For a little while he'd been able to forget his responsibilities and simply enjoy being with her. He'd almost been able to convince himself they were on a kind of date, getting to know one another and having fun. It had been a long time since he'd done that with anyone. He'd forgotten how it felt to spend time free from worry. Though Isabella had always been at the back of his mind. Now he knew she was okay, it seemed that last thread of sanity had snapped. For once he wanted just to act on impulse instead of overanalysing and planning every move. And when Francesca had her body wound around his there was only one thing he could think of.

Their lips still locked together, he backed her into an alcove, out of sight of passers-by. He wanted one moment to enjoy his freedom along with her. His admiration for her had grown over the years, but he'd seen a different side to her tonight. A Francesca free from the restraints of her duty, who allowed herself to show some emotion. The real woman beneath the tiara. It was enough for him to drop his tough exterior and admit how he felt about her. How she made him feel. Like a man who deserved a life of his own.

Everything that had happened tonight had made him reassess his choices. If those affected hadn't held a grudge against him for what had happened, why should he keep holding onto that guilt? All he was doing was punishing himself and no one was benefitting from it. Even though he might not be able to commit to a serious relationship just yet, he could enjoy being with Francesca for a little while longer. It wouldn't be long before they both came to their senses anyway and remembered the positions they held back home. Besides, he knew they could never be together long term anyway. She would marry some day, but she was his in this moment. His heart was safe when they both knew this wasn't going to last.

Francesca definitely wasn't kissing him like a princess. The desire he felt in her every touch making him forget everything about being professional. That ship had sailed the moment he'd planted his lips on hers.

'We're taking a hell of a risk here, Francesca,' he managed to get out through the butterfly kisses with which she was punctuating his every word.

'Why don't we go back to the hotel? We'll have some privacy there.' That fiery passion was there in Francesca's eyes as she made the next move.

Giovanni didn't need asking twice and took her hand to make the way back to the underground station. As buoyed up as he was by the idea of spending the night with her, he also hoping the time it took them to get back to the hotel would wake them out of this lustful daze. Then at least one of them might find the strength to change their mind and put a stop to this before they got in too deep.

He knew sleeping with Francesca would change everything between them, but he couldn't seem to convince himself that this wasn't a good idea. They both wanted this and this was their only chance to be together with no one else around. With no emotional risks involved, because a relationship of any kind beyond this evening of madness was impossible. He could finally let someone close without any fear of commitment and the inevitable loss that surely followed.

Tonight, they were just doing something for themselves, guilt free. Like normal people.

CHAPTER FIVE

BY SUGGESTING THEY take things back to the hotel room, Francesca intimated that she was ready to move on from making out with Giovanni to something more. The only thing that had shocked her more than her own bravado was his willingness to accept the invitation. Clearly their chemistry had taken over from common sense completely, but she wasn't complaining. If this was her only night to be irresponsible and do something crazy, sleeping with her bodyguard was the perfect way to end it.

The station was busy with late-night revellers trying to get home, and when they got on the train there were few seats to be had. She spotted one on the end of the row and pushed Giovanni into it. Not giving him time to protest as she hopped onto his lap, still clutching her teddy bear.

He arched an eyebrow at her. 'What are you doing?'

'Making sure we both have somewhere comfortable to sit.' She leaned in and kissed him full on the mouth.

'Francesca...if you keep doing that it's not going to be comfortable for either of us for very long.' His warning only spurred her on. The sense of power she felt in the knowledge that she could affect the usually cool Giovanni an aphrodisiac in itself.

For once she felt like the one in control in this relationship and intended to take full advantage. She nibbled on his earlobe and he squirmed in his seat, confident he wasn't going to make a scene and draw attention. Though no one seemed to notice anything amiss anyway. The other commuters seemed to have come from a party or festival, all wearing garish outfits and glitter and rhinestones on their faces. Most appeared inebriated or horny, with no interest in Francesca and Giovanni, as they sang and flirted further down the carriage.

Emboldened by her position, and the reversal in their roles, she slipped a hand between their bodies. With her fairground prize hiding her antics from view, she wriggled provocatively in his lap. He jolted beneath her.

'Francesca…' His growled warning made her quiver almost as much as the thick bulge she could feel beneath her.

She gave him a wry smile, watching him fight for control as his jaw tightened.

'We're getting off soon.'

'Already?' She smirked, knowing she was playing with fire. As soon as they were out of sight he'd pay her back.

She was looking forward to it.

Unwilling to embarrass him any further, Francesca managed to keep her hands off him for the duration of their journey and sit still. Though he made sure they were both at the door ready to step off the train well before they reached their final stop. As he marched her through the station, her heart was hammering. She was fuelled by adrenaline and anticipation, knowing he was only just about managing to keep a lid on that simmering passion she'd already had a taste of.

'Are you in a hurry?' she called after him as he blasted his way through the station and out into the dark night.

'Yes.' He pushed her up against the side of the building, taking her breath away as he kissed her hard. If it was meant to be a punishment, her little moan of satisfaction would have told him otherwise.

He hung his head. 'What are you doing to me, Francesca?'

'I would've thought that was obvious.' There was something about this night, being with Giovanni, that made her want to be reckless for once.

'What if we got caught?'

'We won't.'

'I could lose my job.'

'You won't.'

Giovanni let out a long, heavy sigh. 'You don't want this, Francesca. This isn't you.'

It was exactly the thing to say to make her angry. 'You don't know what I want, and you certainly don't know who I am.'

She was fed up with people telling her who she should be instead of letting her just be herself. For one night she'd been able to drop that perfect princess façade, and as far as she was concerned the night wasn't over yet.

'No? So you're not a woman who has spent her whole life pleasing everyone else, and, as much as she thinks she wants to be "normal", would never give up her responsibility as future Queen?' He sounded so smug and self-righteous it should have irked her more than it did. But it seemed he knew her better than anyone.

'Okay, but that doesn't mean I can't have one night off. I'm in a different country, having new experiences. That's not a crime. I just want to have tonight to do what I want, and tomorrow I'll go back to being the model heiress to the throne.'

'Are you suggesting what I think you are?'

Francesca swallowed hard, working up the bravado she would need to pull this off. She wanted Giovanni to think that this was no big deal to her. That he would just be her bit of rough for the night.

'One night together. Free from everything that weighs us both down. Just being us. In the morning we'll go home, and back to the roles we're forced to play.'

If this was her only night to do all the things she had ever wanted, but was too afraid to break any rules, then that included being with Giovanni.

Giovanni hadn't verbally agreed to what Francesca had intimated, but when she'd kissed him again, his body had engaged before his brain had. He wanted her.

And now they were rushing back to the

hotel, hand in hand, Francesca still clutching that ridiculous teddy bear, wearing a plastic tiara on her head. Apparently the sight not any more interesting than regular partygoers as no one batted an eyelid at them. He'd broken all of the rules in the security handbook tonight, but he'd never seen Francesca so happy. Never felt so alive. If one night together was all they could have, he was going to make each second count.

It took every ounce of strength he had waiting for the elevator doors to close, shutting them off from the world, before he kissed her.

'Giovanni...' Francesca dropped her cuddly toy to wrap her arms around him instead and he pulled her flush to his body so he could feel her soft curves against him.

He didn't know if it was because they'd dropped all defences in pursuit of this undeniable passion, or if it was because they both knew this was a one-time deal. But there was a hunger now in their kisses, in their hands exploring one another, that spoke of their urgency to be together.

It was a wrench to break away from her when they arrived at her suite and the door opened.

'Once we do this, there's no going back.' He

was giving her one last chance to change her mind, because he no longer had the strength to deny his feelings for her.

One night would probably never be enough for him. If anything, it would only make it worse for Giovanni, wanting her, knowing he couldn't have her. And yet there was something between them that he'd tried hard to ignore for years. All the times they'd clashed he suspected were out of sheer frustration, denying this attraction between them. Spending time together tonight without outside interference had let it flare to life. It wasn't likely to disappear after sleeping together, but at least they could have one night where they didn't have to pretend those feelings didn't exist. In the end he was going to lose her—to her role as Queen, and to another man—but for tonight she was his.

'Then why are we wasting time talking?' Francesca closed the door behind them and, with one hand on his chest, pushed him back towards the bed.

He liked this side of her. It was honest, real. The confident woman who didn't need anyone to tell her what to do and was quite capable of making her own decisions. He wasn't going to question them again tonight.

He took the plastic tiara from her head and

placed it on the dressing table. 'Not tonight, Princess. I want to be with Francesca.'

That made her smile. 'Good, because I'm tired of being a perfect princess. Tonight I just want to be your lover.'

Francesca tilted her chin up as she always did when she was trying to portray confidence. Biting her lip was the giveaway that she was a little nervous, but then, so was he. He didn't get emotionally involved in the short-lived dalliances he had with the opposite sex. This was different. Francesca and he already had a bond, and he'd shared more with her about his life tonight than he ever had with anyone else. It was going to be difficult to separate the personal and professional side to his relationship with her from now on, but at least they both knew where they stood. After tonight they had to go back to their respective sides on the class divide between royalty and the hired help.

'I like the sound of that.' At least if they went into this with that mindset, that they were just two adults embarking on a night of passion, without any emotional baggage or outside problems, they could enjoy themselves. And each other.

He captured that bottom lip she kept nibbling with his mouth, kissing her softly, letting her know they would take this at her pace. If they only had one night together, he wanted it to be special.

Francesca didn't think she'd ever been this nervous. Not at any royal engagements, or even when she had lost her virginity. She felt more vulnerable because she was doing this with Giovanni as Francesca, not a Princess of Monterossa. Even though she didn't have the eyes of the world on her, she still felt under pressure. To please Giovanni as much as herself. He only had to touch her for her body to go into raptures, and she wanted to do the same for him.

However, she had limited experience, and hadn't had the same emotional connection with Benigno that she had with Giovanni. She'd tried, but obviously she hadn't been able to fake that bond, which came so easily with her protector. At times she'd wondered if she was even capable of feeling so strongly about someone that she could lose all sense like this. Apparently she'd just been with the wrong man.

In hindsight, Benigno had been too much like her. Cosseted his whole life, living in his ivory tower looking down on the world too, he knew nothing of real life either. Could never have given her half of the experiences

Giovanni had given her tonight. Because her feelings for her ex-fiancé had never been as strong as they were for her bodyguard, and Benigno had realised before even she had. He'd resented Giovanni's constant presence in her life, but Francesca had always defended the need to have him there. Even though they'd clashed at times, he was the one steadying presence in her life who never expected anything from her in return.

Perhaps it was just as well that he was out of bounds, when it would be too tempting to lean on him as she had tonight. Then, when he decided, like her parents and Benigno, that she wasn't enough and rejected her too, she'd be devastated. Despite the pain of not being able to be with Giovanni long term, at least she wouldn't have to experience that level of vulnerability unsuitable for a future queen.

Now, she wanted to show him exactly how much he meant to her. As well as fulfilling one of her most erotic fantasies…

Even a kiss from Giovanni was more erotically charged than a night in her ex's bed. She never knew what to expect as he veered between tender and loving, to feverishly passionate. Everything he did causing new sensations to wreak havoc inside her until she was incapable of a coherent thought or staying upright.

Rather than let him think she'd been reduced to a pathetic puddle of need, she backed him towards the bed. Straddling him once he was lying atop the mattress. He seemed content to let her take the lead. For now, at least. It made it easier for Francesca to feel more in control of what she was doing. Even though it was completely out of character for her. Or, perhaps this *was* the real her, and she'd simply never had an opportunity to be herself until now. It had taken Giovanni, a night in London, and finally opening up about how she truly felt for her to truly be herself.

She began to unbutton his shirt, but her trembling fingers weren't co-operating with her seduction plan.

'Let me,' Giovanni said softly, deftly undoing his shirt.

'Sorry.' This wasn't helping her convince him that she would be the kind of woman who could sleep with a man and walk away without giving it a second thought. Probably because it wasn't true.

'Hey, you don't have to prove anything to me.' He reached up and brushed her hair away from her face. Then he kissed her again and she melted into him. Barely noticing, or caring, when he rolled her over so they were lying side by side.

Francesca was more interested in exploring that muscular chest she'd often fantasised about. The smooth taut reality under her fingertips was warm to the touch, reminding her that this was real and no longer merely a dream. She let her hands drift down his torso to the waistband of his trousers, but Giovanni stopped her.

'It's your turn,' he said, lifting her hand to kiss it, putting an end to her exploration for now.

'I might need some help.' Only hours ago Isabella had helped her into this dress, and Francesca had never expected Giovanni would be the one helping her out of it.

She swung her legs over the edge of the bed and sat up so he could reach the zip at the back. He brushed her hair out of the way over her shoulder, and slowly unzipped her, every rasp of the zip, every touch of his fingers on her bare skin, sending her nerve endings haywire. When he finished, he unclasped her bra in one slick movement and pushed her underwear and dress over her shoulders. The cold air on her exposed skin was incredibly arousing. As was the touch of his lips across her back, over her shoulders, and along her neck.

She turned into him, meeting his mouth with hers, as she discarded the rest of her clothes. He cupped her breasts from behind, kneading and squeezing her nipples, flooding her body with arousal.

When Francesca joined him back on the bed he'd stripped off his trousers and was lying there in just his boxer briefs.

'What?' he asked when he saw her wry smile.

'That's just how I pictured you in your underwear.' Black fabric clinging to his sizeable asset and looking sexy as hell.

'Oh? So you've thought about me a lot, then?'

'No.' She was quick with the denial, but could feel the heat in her cheeks giving away the truth. 'Yes.'

Giovanni grinned but gave little away himself. She knew it would eat her up if she didn't ask. 'Did you ever think about me like this?'

She hated to sound needy, and knew she would be despondent if it turned out he hadn't felt the same way up until now, but needed to know the attraction hadn't been one-sided.

He rolled onto his side and fixed her with those intense, deep brown eyes. 'I was afraid to think about this because I knew it would drive me crazy being with you every day. That doesn't mean I didn't admire your courage and strength, or think about how incredibly beautiful you are. I never thought that this, being here with you, was possible.'

He saved himself with the sincerity of his compliments.

'And now?' With the confidence boost, Francesca brazenly pressed her naked body against his.

He palmed her breast possessively. 'Now, you're mine.'

The throbbing need for him inside her began even before he claimed her nipple with his mouth, leaving her gasping. She'd never felt such longing, an actual ache she knew only Giovanni could relieve. But he wasn't ready to pacify her so easily. Instead, he only prolonged the exquisite agony of her wait, attending to that tight bud of sensitive flesh with his tongue. Flicking the tip, teasing it with the graze of his teeth and the rasp of his beard, until she was clutching his hair in her hands, begging him for release.

Though she didn't want him to stop what he was doing either. Her whole body was in turmoil, wanting, enjoying, needing only Giovanni.

She slid her hand back down his body and gripped his erection through the thin fabric of his boxers, enjoying the sharp gasp in response. A taste of his own medicine. Undeterred, she slipped her hand inside and took hold of his thick shaft, though it distracted him momentarily from his own task at hand.

Just as she thought she was getting some relief from the sweet torture, he pulled her flush against him. Pressing the hard evidence of his arousal between her inner thighs.

'Giovanni…' It was a desperate plea. She had waited so long for this moment, for him to give her the release she needed so badly.

'Hold that thought.' When he left her to retrieve a condom from his jacket pocket she thought she was going to pass out from the intensity of that pressure inside her. And he'd barely touched her yet.

She waited not so patiently for him to come back to her, watching his magnificent naked form, and marvelling that he was hers for tonight. Although she tried to relax, it had been a while since she'd shared her body with anyone, and she was tense when he thrust into her.

'Are you okay?' The restraint was there in his quivering voice as he checked on her before going any further.

Francesca bit her lip as she nodded, willing her body not to betray her. To let him know this was more than physical. Her mind fighting against those primal urges, telling her this wasn't a good idea. That one night of passion with Giovanni wasn't something she'd get over easily. More likely it would completely ruin her future prospects for a husband when no other man could hope to compare. Yet he was the one man she couldn't have. At least, not past tonight.

Giovanni took his time kissing her, waiting until she relaxed before he moved inside her again. She felt so full of him that when he withdrew, the loss was immense. Every time he returned to her, relief and pleasure hit all at once.

Sex with Benigno had been perfunctory at best. Something she'd thought she needed to do. It was expected of her, like everything else in her life. She'd wanted to keep her fiancé happy, the relationship important to their families and their country.

This was different. It wasn't just a step-by-step routine to fulfil a need. Or a promise. This was raw passion. Desire. Lust. All things she hadn't thought she would ever get to enjoy. At least not without a scandal. Though she supposed there was still time for that…

Giovanni thrust again with a groan, sending fireworks off in Francesca's head. A celebration of her sensuality and freedom she could feel in every erogenous zone. She was getting close to a feeling she'd never had before, though she'd often professed otherwise with a smile to keep Benigno happy. At the time she'd thought it was her fault, that there was something wrong with her because she couldn't fully give herself to the moment.

It turned out she'd simply been with the wrong man. If she married someone else like Benigno, for all the wrong reasons, she would likely never feel this way again. The most she could hope for in the future was to find someone who respected her half as much as Giovanni. After feeling this way tonight she didn't want to settle for anything less. She hadn't realised how important a satisfying sex life would be to her either. Perhaps this was one area she shouldn't compromise. Something she should have a real say in. After all, it was her body, her heart, that would live with the consequences if she chose the wrong man to spend the rest of her life with again.

If only she could combine Benigno's public standing with everything Giovanni was, she'd have the perfect husband. As it was, she knew she was going to have to hold onto every second, every emotion and physical experience tonight to remember how it felt to simply be herself when free will was taken from her again.

A hungry kiss, a flex of hips, and Giovanni brought her back into the moment with him so she stopped thinking and just enjoyed feeling.

She let Giovanni take her higher and higher, until the world seemed to explode around her and her body shuddered with release. He followed, crying out with a primal roar she suspected he'd needed to let go of for some time. Francesca had a feeling this night had been cathartic for both of them.

Regardless that the future was likely to be more complicated than ever.

Giovanni was no stranger to good sex, but this had been on a different level. Perhaps it was due to years of pent-up feelings, about both Francesca and himself. Tonight had been a journey of discovery for them both. About each other, and themselves.

Nothing was going to change their lives outside this room, but he hoped being honest tonight would help him move on. Especially when it seemed he had the blessing of his old army buddies.

He didn't know what that meant in terms of his future, but for now he was content. Happy. What he did know was that he didn't want this night to ever end.

'Was everything…was I all right?' Francesca was watching him, worrying that sexy bottom lip with her teeth again.

She could obviously tell he had things on his mind, and immediately thought she'd done something wrong. Most likely because that was how she'd been brought up. Always being criticised and told how to do things the 'right way'. Well, he certainly had no complaints about their time together.

'Amazing. Sorry, I'm just thinking about what happens when we go home.'

Francesca screwed up her pretty face. 'Please don't. It'll spoil what little time we have left together.'

He didn't want that either, but there was a concern he'd get carried away by what this meant. It was going to be difficult going back to work, being with her every day, and pretending this hadn't happened. Worse if he did have to watch her meet and fall in love with someone else when he'd just discovered he had feelings for her that obviously went beyond that need to protect her for a pay cheque. It had been bad enough seeing her with Benigno, but now that they'd shared a bed, and so much more, the prospect of seeing her start a life with someone else was going to be hard to stomach.

He'd been trying to keep a lid on the feelings he had for Francesca but tonight had thrown them together closer than ever, and forced him to face how much he liked her. Unfortunately, admitting his feelings didn't guarantee that happy ever after. At least, not for him. He was going to lose her the second they stepped back onto Monterossan soil.

'No regrets?' he asked. He didn't have any at this precise moment, but he had an inkling he might curse himself further down the line for giving into temptation. The memory of sharing this bed haunting him for ever.

How could he go back to nameless, meaningless encounters when he knew what he could really have? A real connection, with emotions involved he didn't think he'd ever share again. Unfortunately, all with the one woman he knew he couldn't have. She was the future Queen of his country, for goodness' sake. The woman he was paid to protect, not sleep with.

'Stop thinking.' She slapped his chest. 'No regrets. Why, have you got any?'

'Definitely not.' That was one thing at least he didn't have to overthink. He wouldn't change anything that had happened tonight for the world.

She let out a long sigh. 'Why can't I just have a normal life?'

'Because you were born for greater things.' He rolled over and kissed her. At least when he was touching her, he didn't have to think about anything else. There wasn't any room for anything else in his head but the taste of her, and how much he wanted her.

He wondered how long he could survive on a diet of sex and Francesca. Actually, on second thought, he didn't care. He'd die a happy man however long it took.

'I can't think of anything better than this,' she murmured contentedly against his lips.

'Nor me. Do you think we can just order room service and live here for ever?' He knew these sweet nothings were simply born of their post-coital bliss, but this room was their safe space. The one place they'd been free to express themselves, and that would all end once they stepped back out of those doors.

'It would be nice, wouldn't it? Do you want

some room service? I've worked up quite a thirst.'

Although he could do with something to drink, Giovanni was reluctant to make the call. 'I don't want to burst our bubble here. Getting room service would require me getting out of your bed and putting on some clothes.'

'You're right. I don't want that either.' Francesca smoothed her hand over his backside before giving it a firm tap. He liked it when she showed a possessive appreciation for his body. Often his looks were the only thing women were interested in, but he knew it was different with Francesca. It had taken a real connection between them to finally act on that physical attraction, and it meant so much more.

The fact that she couldn't keep her hands off him was an extra bonus.

'We do, however, have a fully stocked mini bar, and all the fruit we can possibly eat. I suppose there are some perks to being royalty.' She pulled the sheet off the bed and wrapped it around her, leaving Giovanni lying naked on the bed as she wandered out of the bedroom.

After a moment without her, he decided to go after her and pulled his boxers on to preserve some of his modesty.

'What have you found?'

He found her with her head stuck in the fridge, the light showing the flushed glow on her cheeks after their bedroom workout. She looked the most carefree and happy he'd ever seen her. He couldn't help but wonder if he'd ever get to see her like this again. The only thing worse than thinking it wasn't possible was the thought of someone else making her this happy.

She stood up with her arms full, the sheet tucked carefully toga-style to leave her hands free. Hair mussed, lipstick smudged, she was as far as she could possibly get from the tabloid image of the Princess of Monterossa. This was his Francesca. Even if it was just for tonight.

'We've got wine, crisps, nuts, chocolate… all the things I'm not supposed to eat if I want to keep my figure.' She rolled her eyes and he guessed that was a statement she'd heard many times from her 'advisors'. He'd certainly been privy to some conversations that had made him want to step in when stylists and the like had treated her like a clothes horse rather than a human being.

'I thought we'd established that none of the usual rules apply tonight.' He wrapped his arms around her and nibbled the skin at her neck.

'In that case I'm going to be really wicked.'

Before he got his hopes up for an extra round in the bedroom, she deposited her goodies on the glass table in the luxurious lounge area. It never failed to amuse him that in his line of work he got to see how the other half really lived. Private pools and presidential suites were a far cry from the stark army barracks that he'd lived in after his parents' deaths.

Even now, when he was old enough and could afford his own place, it was a modest apartment close to the palace so he was always on call for duty. He didn't spend much time there so there had never been a need to splash the cash on expensive furnishings like those Francesca and her family were used to. The gilded mirrors and sparkling crystal chandeliers were another reminder that he and Francesca were worlds apart.

'I need a drink.' Alcohol preferably, to make him forget that he'd put his job and everything else on the line by being with her like this. Though, it was worth it.

Francesca poured two glasses of wine and beckoned him over to sit with her in front of the full-length windows, the city at night providing the view for their late-night picnic. Rather than sit in any of the well-upholstered wingback chairs, she'd chosen to sit cross-legged on the floor. Another moment of rebellion, he supposed. It occurred to him in that moment that perhaps that was all he'd been, too. Francesca sticking her two fingers up at her social standing by sleeping with the hired help. Something that didn't sit well with him when he knew he'd had altogether different reasons for bedding her.

Francesca had added the overflowing fruit bowl to their supplies and was currently enjoying the strawberries along with her wine. 'I hope wherever Isabella is, she's having as much of a good time as I am.'

'Do you? Really?' Giovanni raised his eyebrows, sure that if Isabella had been up to half of what they'd done tonight Francesca would've had a conniption.

She thought about it for a moment. 'Within reason. As long as nobody gets hurt, and nobody finds out.'

He knew that went for them too. They hadn't exactly been discreet, despite their concerns at the start of the evening. It had been easy to get complacent as the barriers between them had fallen. Though at this moment he didn't think either of them particularly cared. That was a worry for tomorrow. Or, as he checked his watch, later today. It was tempting to stay up all night and eke out every last second of this time with Francesca.

Giovanni helped himself to some very fine chocolate and broke a piece off for Francesca, who took it directly from his fingers with her mouth. An intimate act that aroused more than a passing interest. Especially since she took her time, slowly and deliberately prolonging the exchange, her eyes not leaving his. A hunger blazing there for more than all the chocolate and strawberries in the world.

He stopped pretending he wanted anything other than her to eat, pushing everything aside, not caring what spilled, as he pulled her towards him. Francesca's eyes blazed with an already familiar passion, encouraging him more. He wrenched the sheet away, exposing her body, and, with a predator-like crawl, covered her body with his until she was lying flat on the floor. Her naked breasts rose and fell with her every shallow breath as she waited for his next move.

Giovanni took one of the strawberries from the fruit bowl between his teeth and began tracing it along all the soft, sensitive parts of her body. He started between her legs, up along her inner thigh, dipping into that most intimate part of her to make her gasp. On he went, the sensation causing her to contract her stomach muscles and he remembered she was ticklish there. He carried on, leaving a trail of strawberry juice over her breast, and around her nipples. Enjoying her squirm and make little meowing noises beneath him. When he finally brought it to her lips she bit down, the juices running down her chin and neck as they consumed the fruit between them.

He licked the tart but sweet trail, travelling back down her body.

'I'm all sticky.' She giggled as he swirled his tongue around her nipples.

'Just how I like you.'

Down he travelled until his head was buried between her legs and he lapped her sweet juices, enjoying her moans of ecstasy. He felt her body convulse around him as he brought her to the edge of orgasm on the tip of his tongue. And when she spilled over, Giovanni was almost ready to go with her.

He waited until she'd come back down to earth and was able to breathe again before he attempted conversation.

'Are you okay?'

Her grin told him all he needed to know. 'More than okay.'

'In that case, can we take this back to the

bedroom? I don't want to be lying here in full view of the great British public when the sun comes up.' Though he didn't want to say it, he wanted their last few hours together to be spent in bed, where he could have her in his arms in comfort.

CHAPTER SIX

FRANCESCA STRETCHED AND smiled before she even opened her eyes. The night had been the best of her life and she didn't want to admit it was over.

She was even more bereft than anticipated when she did finally look around, only to find the other side of the bed empty. The dream was definitely over. She grabbed the pillow, which still smelled of Giovanni, and placed it over her head, trying to stay firmly in denial. If he was gone already, their time together was at an end and once she got out of this bed it was business as usual. A difficult thing to come to terms with after spending the night pretty much doing what she wanted.

'I've ordered some room service for you, but I'm heading out to pick up Isabella. She's staying at another hotel nearby.' The sound of Giovanni's voice coaxed her out from her pillow cocoon.

He was already showered and dressed and back to his polished, professional self. As handsome as he was, Francesca preferred him a little more unbuttoned.

'Have you heard from her? Who is she with?' She couldn't help but think if her sister had chosen to stay at a different hotel, it meant she'd spent the night with someone. Likely a man. And goodness knew if he was going to be discreet about whatever had taken place between them. All she could do was trust Isabella hadn't picked someone entirely unsuitable to entertain her romantic fantasies.

She wasn't a hypocrite. Hooking up with Giovanni likely hadn't been the best idea for her either, but at least he could be trusted to keep the details to himself. All they needed was someone keen to make a name for themselves, or looking to make a few pounds from the tabloids, and their cover was well and truly blown. Not to mention Isabella's reputation.

'I just got the message to go and pick her up. You two should probably talk if you want the details. It's not my place.' His face was set in steel, giving nothing away about their tryst only hours ago in this bed, and on the lounge floor.

'Giovanni, we need to talk about what happened between us.' She had hoped they'd have some time together before they had to go home, where they really wouldn't have any privacy to dissect the events of the previous night. Although they wouldn't have a chance to explore any kind of relationship, she would've liked to at least talk about where they went from here. He was still going to be in her life and it was going to be difficult pretending nothing had happened. Although he seemed to be doing a pretty good job of it so far.

He dropped his head, letting the façade of the cool and collected bodyguard slip a little. 'I know, but not now. I need to go and get your sister and exert some damage control if necessary. I promise we'll have a chat, but I still have a job to do, Francesca.'

'I know.' More was the pity. She could have quite happily spent the rest of her days in this hotel room with him and forgotten about the rest of the world.

He crossed the room in a couple of strides and came to her side of the bed. 'Last night meant a lot to me, Francesca.'

He dropped a kiss on her forehead, and she had a feeling he wanted to say more. Something she probably didn't want to hear right now, but which they both knew was inevitable.

All she could do was let him go, and pray their escapades in London weren't going to come back and bite them all on the backside.

Francesca tried to keep herself busy until Giovanni and Isabella returned. Although she was hungry, her churning stomach wouldn't let her eat more than a few bites of toast and some orange juice. Regardless that Giovanni appeared to have ordered enough food to feed a small army. She used the time to try and make herself presentable, transforming herself from the wanton she'd been last night to the picture-perfect princess for any waiting press.

After her shower, she changed into a stylish pale blue coat dress with contrasting white buttons, and a sash belt tied at her waist. An outfit that had been chosen before she'd even left Monterossa and probably cost a fortune. Though as far as she was concerned, the outfit she'd returned to the hotel in last night was worth a lot more. She stroked her hand over the torn dress she lifted from the floor, caught sight of the shoes customised courtesy of Giovanni. They represented the spontaneous nature of their adventures perfectly, and to her they were priceless. When her things were packed for the journey home, they would be the first to go in her case.

Before Isabella, or anyone else, came into the lounge area, she made sure to clear away all evidence of her and Giovanni's carpet picnic at the window. In the light of day she could see what a chance they'd taken of being seen. Even though they were twenty storeys up, the entire city centre was visible below them. Who knew if anyone could actually see into the room? Now she was back into her royal role, her paranoia had flared back into life. It had been nice to take a risk or two, but now she had to fall into line.

It didn't matter about the passion he'd awakened inside her, or what her heart wanted. Once they left this hotel room she had to resume her 'perfect princess' role and that did not include causing a scandal by getting caught in a compromising position with her bodyguard. Her public profile had to take priority over her desires or she would lose support on a grand scale. It was necessary to leave last night behind her if she was ever going to move on and marry as expected.

She threw the rubbish and leftover snacks in the bin, set the glasses to the side, and lifted the sheet she'd discarded on the floor to take back into the bedroom. The sight of it brought back some heat-inducing memories. What Giovanni had done to her, what they'd done together, had been beyond her imagination, and she wished that it didn't have to end here and now.

Francesca had spent so much of her life doing the right thing by everyone, and seeing how different her life could've been was as much of a curse as a good time. Now she knew how it felt to be with Giovanni, to have a more than satisfying sex life, and to be able to express herself without censorship, it was tough to leave all of that behind.

How could she walk into an arranged marriage when she clearly had feelings for someone else? Someone who was still going to be in her life every day. Worse, how was she going to share a bed with anyone else when her heart, along with every other part of her body, belonged to Giovanni? It seemed marriage was going to be even more of a prison than life at the palace. One with added torture.

Before she could get too maudlin, mourning a life she could never have with the man who'd opened her eyes to so much last night, Giovanni returned with Isabella in tow and her relief at seeing her sister overtook everything. Right before the anger kicked in.

'Where have you been? Where on earth were you? Are you safe?' Francesca had her by the shoulders, desperately searching to see if she'd suffered any physical injuries.

'Yes, yes, I'm safe. I was…a few places.'

Eventually Isabella admitted she'd spent the night with Rowan James. The ex who'd called off the wedding, leaving Isabella broken hearted.

Francesca couldn't believe she'd been so reckless. Though she supposed if Isabella had been here last night, she wouldn't have been able to do half the things she'd done with Giovanni. Still, as the older sister it was her right to be annoyed at her little sister going AWOL in the middle of the night.

Flashes of London last night came to mind. Being on the underground, eating fast food in the street, having fun at the fairground— all with Giovanni, under the guise of looking for her sister. She was angry, not only at Isabella for putting them all in danger, but at herself for forgetting about Isabella at times when she had been so caught up in Giovanni's attention. Mostly, she was angry that they had to be sneaky to have a night doing what everyone else in the world took for granted.

Isabella apologised for leaving her shoes be-

hind and making her worry she'd been kid-
napped. For not staying in contact. For making
her go to Twilight in the first place. For everything.

And then she burst into tears.

'It's all right.' Francesca folded her sister into
her arms. 'We're both to blame. I guess we
needed to let off some steam last night.' She
glanced at Giovanni, who made brief eye contact before looking away again. A silent, neu-
tral sentry. Nothing like the man she'd shared
a bed with just this morning.

'You don't understand… I hadn't planned
any of it. Believe it or not, I was trying to stay
out of trouble.' Through her sobs, it was clear
Isabella had a lot to tell her.

It seemed wrong to hear her confession in
front of the man Francesca had sinned with
herself. She felt enough of a hypocrite without
having Giovanni witness it.

'Okay. Why don't you tell me about it whilst
we go and get you freshened up?' Francesca led
a clearly distraught Isabella to the bathroom.
Whatever had occurred between her and her
ex mustn't have ended well given her current
state. Francesca's upset at having her time with
Giovanni curtailed paled into comparison next
to her sister's distress. She'd had an actual re-

lationship with Rowan; nearly married him. There was no way she would've spent the night with him unless something significant had happened between them. Yet, there was no sign of him now. The fact that he wasn't here to see them off back home, or to try and persuade Isabella to stay with him, spoke volumes. She'd had more heartbreak.

Francesca taking out her frustrations on her too wasn't going to help her current mood or get her to open up. For everyone's sake she was going to have to find out what happened and figure out a way for everyone to leave London with their reputations intact. Even if their hearts were more than a little bruised by everything they had to leave behind.

She was going home with a lot more than a tacky snow globe with a London landmark inside that tourists usually brought home as a souvenir. Thanks to her night off from being a princess, she was taking back deeper feelings for her bodyguard than a simple crush, and an existential crisis about her future as Queen.

Giovanni was trying not to listen to Francesca and Isabella's heart-to-heart on the plane, though it wasn't easy in the close confines of the cabin. He was supposed to stay close, and objective, at all times after all. Needless to say, it involved a lot of tears from Isabella, who'd apparently spent the night with her ex. The one who'd hurt the family with the scandal before the wedding that never was. Or one of the weddings that had been called off. The Princesses really deserved better, and appeared to have appalling taste in men. He included himself in that category when he was probably the last person on earth Francesca should've bedded.

Though he couldn't bring himself to regret anything that had happened when they'd been so good together.

It just made things all that more complicated when they got home.

He had to admit, though, he was beginning to have some empathy with Isabella's ex. It wasn't easy being involved with the family. Impossible to have the sort of normal relationship he longed for in his post-sex delirium when anything seemed within his reach. Even happiness. Only news of Isabella's whereabouts first thing had jolted him back to reality, reminding him he had a job to do. And, if he wasn't more careful, Francesca was going to end up another casualty of the curse. By getting close to him she'd put herself at serious risk, which, although not physically dangerous, left her open to hurt in other ways. In reputation and her relationship with her family.

They had agreed that last night had to be put firmly in the past so they could carry on with their lives as they were. Yet, the way she kept stealing glances at him gave him the impression they weren't done just yet. He supposed she had said she wanted to at least discuss what had happened. Goodness knew what that was supposed to achieve other than make them both yearn for a repeat of last night.

The mere memory of her touch, her taste, and sleeping with her in his arms was enough to make him forget his position. Leaving her this morning was one of the hardest things he'd ever had to do, but he'd had to put his duty above his heart. Giving him some idea of what Francesca had to go through. It was torturous.

He held his tongue until Isabella seemed to have cried herself to sleep, and Francesca got up from her seat to go to the bathroom.

'Francesca—'

He stopped her in the small alcove at the back of the plane, away from prying eyes and listening ears, before she went back to her seat.

When she looked up at him, that amber gaze so full of yearning, he couldn't help but reach out and touch her. She closed her eyes as he brushed his knuckles against her cheek, and Giovanni was tempted to cart her back into the bathroom for one last hurrah before they reached home. Unfortunately joining the mile high club wasn't going to make any of this easier for either of them.

He cleared his throat and did his best to rid himself of thoughts unbecoming to a personal protection officer assigned to the princess he was fantasising about.

And failed.

Instead, he unfurled his fingers and cupped her face. 'I miss you already.'

When she did venture to look at him again, it was easy to see she felt the same. How they were going to conceal their secret from her parents, he didn't know.

'Me too, but we can't go back no matter how much we might want to.'

There was no 'might' about it. If he could relive last night ad infinitum he'd be a happy man. But she was right, they couldn't possibly pick up from where they'd left off last night. Even if they'd been denied time together this morning.

Still, they weren't back on home soil just yet.

'No, but I don't think we got to say one last goodbye, did we? How can we possibly have closure without that?' He brushed his thumb over her full lips, mesmerised by the memory of how soft and pliant they were against his.

'Indeed.'

If he'd been expecting Francesca would be the one to see sense and bat away his advances, he was mistaken. In fact, she was moving closer, closing the slight distance between them. Until all that was keeping their lips apart was his thumb. A matter he took care of quickly.

One soft kiss. A goodbye, and a return to their normal status quo. That had been his intention. However, the second their lips met it seemed as though they'd once again set events in motion that even they had no control over. Their mouths clashed together with an urgency that hadn't been present last night. They didn't have the luxury of time or privacy here on the plane to indulge this chemistry that had finally been allowed to be unleashed after years of being suppressed. Now it seemed it was going to be impossible to put the lid back on it.

Though he was aware that the rest of the Princesses' entourage was sitting at the back of the plane, and he didn't want to compromise her any more than she already might be, he backed them both into the bathroom, locking the door behind them. Their lips not parting from one another.

'Do you have any contraception?' It was Francesca who finally broke away.

He nodded and produced a condom from his wallet. 'Are you sure you want to do this? Here?'

'Why not? We may as well end things with a bang.' She had a wicked smile when she was being un-princess-like. Giovanni liked this wild side of Francesca that no one else got to see and reap the benefits from.

He grabbed her backside and lifted her onto the dressing table. Thankfully the bathroom on a royal jet was more spacious than the standard commercial airline, so they were afforded a little luxury.

As much as he wanted to rip her dress open, buttons scattered to the floor in his haste, he was aware Francesca's appearance on arrival would be scrutinised as always. So he carefully unbuttoned her all the way down the front, watching her chest rise and fall as he slowly undid her belt, and let her dress fall open.

He took in the sight of the lacy white underwear against her tanned skin in case it was the last time he got to see her like this. Wanting, needing, only him.

He kissed her hard, Francesca already unzipping his fly and urging him on. Following her lead, he quickly divested her of her panties, before sheathing himself. It was a struggle to contain himself when he entered her in one quick thrust. The overwhelming natural response to cry out his instant satisfaction only quelled by the thought of everyone else outside the door.

Francesca, on the other hand, seemed unable to suppress her delight, her little moans of appreciation, which he'd so enjoyed last night, now in danger of giving them away.

'Shh. Someone's going to hear you.' He tried to quiet her, but every tilt of his hips against her, bringing their bodies together, seemed to make her more vocal.

In the end he resorted to putting a hand over her mouth to quiet her. A move that served to make her eyes sparkle with mischief as she licked and nibbled at his palm. That touch of her tongue on his skin heightened his arousal, increasing his pace in search of that final release.

Francesca wrapped her legs around his waist, tightened her hold inwardly too, until he was consumed by his need to let go completely. Then she pulled his hand away from her mouth, leaned in and sucked on the skin at the base of his neck. That pleasurable pain and further display of her wild side sufficient for him to lose the last of his control. He had to bury his head in the crook of Francesca's neck so he didn't roar the place down, and when she climaxed too, he had to cover her mouth again.

His exertions left him gasping for breath and he all but collapsed on top of her, his jelly-like legs struggling to keep him upright. Francesca had a devastating impact on him both physically and emotionally, but he'd never felt so alive.

It was a shame this was their goodbye.

CHAPTER SEVEN

'FRANCESCA? IS EVERYTHING all right?' Isabella knocked on the bathroom door and sent Francesca and Giovanni into a tizzy of trying to rearrange their clothes and not get caught out.

'I—I'm not feeling very well. Could you ask someone to get me a glass of water, please?' Still struggling to get her breathing under control, and panicking that her sister was about to figure out what she'd been doing in the bathroom with their security detail, Francesca tried desperately to buy them some time.

The reflection of her flushed face in the mirror, along with her partially naked body, would definitely give the game away. At least Giovanni had managed to make himself look respectable in double-quick time, despite ravishing her so thoroughly. She was afraid her vocal satisfaction had drawn some attention after getting carried away in the moment.

'I'll go and get it myself. It's probably all the

stress I've caused, making you unwell.' Isabella's contriteness made her grimace in the face of her fib. Lying to her sister wasn't something she did easily, but in this instance it would save them all from further embarrassment, as well as keep Giovanni in his job.

'Thank you,' she said, meekly. 'I'll be out in a moment.'

Once the sound of Isabella's footsteps receded down the aisle, Francesca opened the door slightly to check the coast was clear. 'You should go now before anyone sees.'

'We still haven't had the chance to talk,' Giovanni reminded her with a grin.

'Later. Go.' She ushered him out, and just when she thought they were safe, he ducked his head back in through the door and kissed her thoroughly. Leaving her dazed and wanting more.

'Later.' He gave her a wink and disappeared to the rear of the craft, leaving the coast clear.

Francesca took a moment to compose herself. Fixing her hair back in place, and splashing some cold water on her face, to take away the look of impropriety. Though she couldn't resist a sly smile at her reflection. This certainly had been an interesting, if unexpected, turn of events making an otherwise tiring flight into something exhilarating.

It seemed they couldn't be alone without giving into that passion that flared so easily to life between them. A matter that was going to make life tricky at the palace. Though they'd agreed that their escapades should end once they were back on home ground, their 'eventful' use of alone time meant they would have to raise the subject of their night in London at a later stage. Carrying it over the border into real life in Monterossa. And now they had another indiscretion to add to the list of topics they needed to discuss.

She ran into Isabella as she exited the bathroom.

'Come and sit down. Would you like me to inform the pilot? He can radio ahead for medical assistance, or divert us to a closer airport.' Isabella's concern was touching, but only made Franccsca fccl more wretched about her ruse.

This was partly why she and Giovanni couldn't carry on their 'arrangement' at home. It was one thing being anonymous and alone in London, where no one else was concerned about what they got up to. But it would take a certain level of subterfuge to keep seeing each other, involving lots more lying to her family, as well as increased personal risk involving his job and her reputation. She wouldn't be such a good match for a well-heeled gentleman if she was involved in yet another romance scandal. Sleeping with the hired help would seem tawdry for a woman of her standing, even in this day and age.

Giovanni wasn't promising her for ever, and having a relationship meant risking her entire future as well as her position in the family. He would probably tire of her like everyone else and where would that leave her? As much as she wanted to be with him, she had to be logical. Practical. Being Queen was the only future she could count on. She needed someone who could present that perfect façade with her, and who wouldn't distract her. Take a piece of her heart when she needed to give it entirely to her country.

'That's really not necessary. I'll be all right once I sit down and have some water.' Guilt wouldn't let Francesca accept her sister's fussing, not to mention inconveniencing everyone else just to cover up her dalliance with Giovanni.

She took a seat in the luxurious, spacious area reserved for the family and their security. Thankfully Giovanni had made himself scarce for now so she could try and think clearly without images of him, head buried in her shoulder as he climaxed, dominating her thoughts.

Isabella threw herself down into a neighbouring chair with a sigh. Clearly, there was something other than her sister's well-being on her mind.

'What's bothering you, Bella?'

Isabella stared at the hands resting in her lap for some time before answering. 'Last night wasn't just about meeting up with Rowan. There was a photographer—'

Francesca's heart plummeted into her stomach. Those feel-good endorphins Giovanni had whipped up inside her fast becoming a distant memory. 'Who? What? Where?'

More importantly, what exactly had they captured? She was sure between them she and Isabella had provided plenty of salacious photo ops. There were some innocent moments with Giovanni, which could probably be explained away, but there was also the matter of them naked in full view of the city last night in the hotel room. Now she was beginning to feel genuinely ill.

Tears, it seemed, were never too far from Isabella's eyes since they'd left London. 'It was a photograph of Rowan and I in a...compromising position. We spent most of the night chasing down the owner of the paper to beg him not to publish it.'

'And?' Francesca wished she'd asked for something stronger than water. Though glad it wasn't incriminating evidence of her rash behaviour with Giovanni, she didn't wish her sister's name to be sullied further either.

Isabella screwed up her face, and Francesca's stomach almost made a leap for freedom too.

'We had to come to an arrangement in exchange for them not publishing the photograph.'

'What kind of "arrangement"?' She had a feeling she wasn't going to like it even though it had to be preferable to Isabella being on the front page.

'Rowan and I have agreed to give an exclusive interview.'

'Why would they want to interview a couple who've already broken up?'

'Because they want the juicy details. Because they want the credit for breaking the story, and now, perhaps, they think they're going to get an exclusive that we're back together.'

'And are you?' Certainly, spending the night together would have suggested that, but Francesca didn't think her sister's tears had come from simply saying goodbye to Rowan until their next meet.

Isabella shook her head, dislodging some of those leftover tears. 'No. We made a mistake last night. One that's not going to be repeated.'

Francesca felt for her in that moment. Knew exactly what it was to have that one night of surety, only to realise in the cold light of day that being with someone from such a different background simply wasn't feasible.

She moved over onto Isabella's seat and wrapped her arms around her sister. 'It's not easy, is it?'

'What?'

'Falling for someone you can't be with.' Francesca sighed as Giovanni strode into the cabin on his way to the cockpit to check in with the pilot.

Isabella followed her gaze. 'Oh, my goodness! You and Giovanni?'

'What? No. What makes you say that?' Francesca spluttered, knowing she'd stuffed up. She'd been too blasé about the whole thing, and Isabella had sussed what was going on between them within a matter of hours. How the hell was she going to keep it secret from her parents and everyone else when they were going to be together every day? Especially when they didn't appear able to keep their hands off one another.

'Er, the way you're mooning after him. I was too caught up in my own complicated feelings about Rowan to notice before, but there is definitely a vibe between you both. Now I come to think of it, he seemed grumpier than usual this morning. I assumed it was because I'd caused him a security nightmare, but now I'm wondering if it was because I got him out of your bed this morning.'

Francesca neither confirmed nor denied the accusation.

Isabella's eyes went wide as saucers. 'I'm right, aren't I? I want *all* the details.'

Apparently Francesca's face had done all the talking, and now she was sure she was scarlet at being found out. The whole reasoning behind her and Giovanni giving in to temptation was because no one would know. It was supposed to be a secret just between the two of them. How long that was going to last there was no way of telling.

'We both acted out of character last night, Bella. Let's just leave it at that.'

'No way. Here I am pouring my heart out to you, blaming myself for causing everyone so much stress, and all the time you were otherwise engaged. With your bodyguard.' She shook her head, and Francesca knew she was disappointed in her behaviour.

Once they were back home, Isabella wasn't going to be the only one.

'It was a one-off. Never going to happen again. Not worth mentioning.' More lies. It had already happened a second, now a third, time and it was definitely worth shouting from the rooftops if it wouldn't put her entire future as Queen in jeopardy.

Isabella continued to stare at her, and Francesca did her best not to react. Even as Giovanni passed back through the cabin.

'So what's going to happen once you get home?' Isabella whispered.

'Nothing. I told you. It's over and done with. Back to normal as soon as we land. Now, enough about my mistakes, what are you going to do about Rowan?' It was playing dirty perhaps to put the ball back in her sister's court, but Francesca didn't want to examine everything that had happened with Giovanni with her. Mostly because she was afraid she was already in too deep, and didn't know how she was going to move past it.

Isabella shrugged. 'There's not much I can

do. We have to give this interview, then I guess it's back to normal.'

Francesca recognised the pain and uncertainty in her sister's eyes because she was feeling the same way as Monterossa came into view below them. Their plans to have one night of being 'normal' had completely backfired, leaving them more conflicted than usual about their lives at the palace. And the relationships they'd left behind in London.

Though Francesca had returned home to freshen up first, Isabella had gone on ahead to the hospital to speak to their parents about Rowan and the upcoming interview. She'd decided to be upfront about what had happened in London. To a point. Francesca suspected her sister left some of the more lurid details out. As would she.

Thanks to Isabella's confession that they had ditched the party and had a night in the city, she was sure she'd be in for a grilling from her parents. Not to mention a stern ticking-off. But there were some things they were better off not knowing. It wouldn't achieve anything by letting them know she'd spent the night with her bodyguard, except a lot of disappointment, worry, and Giovanni likely losing his job.

They'd gone to a lot of trouble to cover their tracks, but she understood her sister's need to confess. Guilt was a terrible burden. Giovanni was proof enough of how it could destroy a person's life, and she didn't wish that on her sister. Secrets had a way of eventually coming to the surface anyway. It had barely been twenty-four hours since she and Giovanni had shared one and it had already been uncovered by Isabella.

Of course, Giovanni had escorted her to the hospital, but they hadn't yet had a moment alone. Even now he was outside her father's room conversing with the other security detail. No doubt making plans for when the King was discharged home. She realised now how much planning went into their every move, and why they needed it. Without Giovanni's guidance in London, things could've turned out very badly for her. Naïve, alone, and without the foresight to even carry any cash, that had been her first risk. Sleeping with Giovanni had been her second. Not because it put her in harm's way, but because she'd endangered her heart.

'It's so good to see you.' Francesca kissed her parents on the cheek. Her stomach rolling at the prospect of this conversation. As ridiculous as it was to be afraid of her parents' wrath at this age, it had been uppermost in her mind since London. Especially when she knew Isabella had already told them of her failings.

No doubt they would blame her for the events that had unfolded because she should have known better. She was the one who had most to lose by running wild in public. Being at the coronation should have reminded her of her duty. Unfortunately, it had only reminded her of the lack of control she had over her own life.

If she was honest, she still held some resentment. Mostly about not being able to be with Giovanni. Someone from a normal family wouldn't have any trouble pursuing a relationship with someone she had an incredible bond with. But she didn't have the luxury of exploring anything with Giovanni publicly.

She couldn't bring herself to say it was good to be home because that meant saying goodbye to the freedom she'd so enjoyed with Giovanni.

'I hear you had fun in London.' Her father gave her a pointed look and she hung her head like a scolded child.

'I'm sorry. I should've known better. It won't happen again.' She didn't know what else she could say, knowing she'd let the family down with her wayward behaviour.

'We're very disappointed in you, Francesca.' Her mother's sharp tone made her wince.

She knew she'd let them down, but hearing it come from them struck her deep in the heart.

'I know.' Nothing she could say would ever make up for what she had done. Even if she could find the words to express her remorse for letting them down.

'You're going to be Queen some day. You can't afford to be seen falling out of clubs, or acting irresponsibly. The whole country needs to believe you're capable of being a leader. That you're not just a privileged princess taking her position for granted. You need public support and you're not going to have that if you embarrass us all abroad. Now, more than ever, your reputation needs to be pristine. You represent Monterossa, Francesca.' Her father's face was sterner than she'd ever seen, and she was devastated that she'd caused them this much anguish.

She'd spent a lifetime trying to gain their approval and she'd stuffed everything up with one stupid mistake. There had been small misdemeanours in the past when she'd forgotten certain protocols in public when her parents had admonished her, reminded her of correct etiquette. This was on a different level. And she hated the look of disappointment she saw reflected in their eyes.

'I'm sorry. I'll do better.' Her voice was small, though she was determined to prove herself worthy of her place in the family now more than ever.

She'd made one slip-up, which they'd hopefully look past as long as she did her best to live up to their expectations. With no more room for mistakes.

The King beckoned her over to his bedside and took her hand. 'I understand the pressure you are under as the next in line to the throne, daughter. I was there myself once too. I remember that urge to run and hide from my duty, but it is not a luxury either of us can afford to indulge. I trust now that you've got that out of your system, we can expect you to return to being the loyal Princess of Monterossa who we know and love?'

He raised an eyebrow at her to let her know exactly what was expected of her. She wanted to replace the frowns and scowls on their faces with beaming smiles. Pride.

'Of course. Thank you for being so understanding, Father.' She had to accept her fate was to eventually rule the country, and with the privileges she so enjoyed came the responsibility she was born into. There was no getting around that. There was no room for anyone, or anything, else. Including Giovanni.

At least she'd had London.

'With your father getting out of hospital soon, we've decided to go away for a few days so he can recuperate,' her mother interjected.

'Good idea. I wouldn't recommend London for a relaxing break though. In my experience, it can get a bit hectic.' Some day she knew she'd look back on it and think it was probably the best time of her life. Once the worry about Isabella and Rowan dissipated, and her own dalliance with Giovanni was likely a distant memory, she'd remember how free she'd felt. Uninhibited. Normal. Everything she'd wanted to experience, and more. The most exciting night she knew she'd never forget.

'No, we're planning on doing a little less... socialising.' Though her mother's carefully chosen words were probably referencing her sister's time with Rowan, Francesca couldn't help but think about Giovanni and what her parents would think if they knew what had happened between them.

Their parents had been very accommodating at the time of Isabella's engagement, given Rowan's very different background. Likely because the King had married a commoner too.

An actress no less! The fact that their mother, Gloria, had been a Hollywood star had probably given them more kudos. However, Francesca was the future Queen. Even if her parents did accept him as a suitable match, there wouldn't be room for a husband, or anything, other than her duty to her country. She had feelings for Giovanni, but he needed someone who was going to be there for him. He needed a wife, not a queen. Not that either of them was even thinking about marriage...

'We want you to take the reins for a little while in my place. Hopefully it won't be a permanent arrangement, but we thought perhaps now was the time for you to step forward and assume more royal duties. I'm not physically able at the minute, and I think it will help your credibility to be more visible in my absence.' As usual, her father was very matter-of-fact, and she didn't have to try very hard to read between the lines.

He wanted her to prove herself. Understandable, given the circumstances, along with her recent behaviour. Not only did he have his own health struggles, but she'd dropped the ball when he was most likely hoping she was ready to take over when the time came.

So was she. Francesca knew she was capable, but she would admit that recently she'd questioned if it was a role she really wanted. Being Queen meant giving up any thoughts of ever having a life of her own. Being with Giovanni in London had given her a glimpse of that parallel universe where she had no responsibilities, and was free to do whatever, be with whoever she wanted. It was akin to having cold feet before your wedding day. Except the repercussions for Francesca would be so much more than a distraught groom if she decided not to go through with her big day. She'd already let her family down, and she felt awful. Without their faith and support, she had nothing. And she would only have that as long as she proved she was still their perfect princess.

'Of course. I will liaise with everyone to take over your royal duties for now so you can recover. We need you fit and well.' Hopefully to return to the throne where he belonged. Francesca wasn't ready to lose him, or to follow in his footsteps just yet.

'Thank you, Francesca. We know we can rely on you.' Her mother put her hand on her arm and gave her a squeeze.

Francesca swallowed the sudden ball of fear in her throat and forced a smile.

She supposed in the circumstances she and

Isabella had got off lightly. For two people who'd always been so strict about how their children should act in public, her parents were surprisingly calm about their daughters going rogue in another country. Especially when there apparently was photographic evidence of at least one of them.

At least they were giving her a second chance. To prove her worth as Queen. To do the right thing. To put everything that had happened in London behind her. Including sleeping with Giovanni. He was a temptation she couldn't afford to give into again.

CHAPTER EIGHT

'I DON'T SEE why I have to go.' Giovanni understood why Francesca had distanced herself from him since their return. Even why she'd been colder towards him after speaking to her parents. However, he didn't understand why she felt the need to punish him.

Thankfully, she apparently hadn't told her parents everything that had happened in London as he still held his position at the palace. Something that was now under threat with this particular senior royal.

'It's not that I'm firing you, Giovanni. You're just moving to another team. I think there's too much baggage between us now to carry on. My parents have given me an opportunity to show the country I'm a natural successor to their King, and I can't have anything jeopardising that. And, please, I think it's better that you address me by my proper title from now on. I think being too familiar is exactly why I should appoint someone else as my personal protection officer. How can you be subjective in your job when we have a...history?' As she stumbled over the last word, it betrayed the cool, calm demeanour she'd displayed since calling him into the study to talk to him in private.

With her parents gone, and taking on more royal duties, she needed him more than ever, but she was trying to tell him otherwise.

'You know I'm good at my job, *Your Highness*. I would never let anything get in the way of your safety. I can assure you of that.' He was trying to keep the anger out of his voice, but it wasn't easy when she was threatening to replace him. Especially when it wasn't his capability in question.

He had wondered how they were going to work together after everything that had happened, but he hadn't anticipated the prospect of losing her altogether. Now she was apparently expecting him to move away and leave her safety in someone else's hands. Not an easy thing for him to do when looking after her had been his sole purpose for so long. This wasn't just a job to him. Certainly now that they'd forged such a bond. And he couldn't trust anyone else to keep her safe the way he had. No one could possibly care for her more than he did.

'I don't think either of us were particularly professional in London, and I can't afford any more mistakes.'

That one hurt. Almost as much as when he'd heard her telling Isabella that their time together meant nothing. The fact that she didn't want him in charge of her personal safety suggested it might be more.

Of course she might have had regrets, but then they'd indulged their carnal urges on the plane as well. Now he wondered if she was simply afraid of them continuing to work together in case it happened again.

Since she had referenced their personal relationship, he thought it safe to talk about it. Regardless that they'd avoided it for the few days since they'd been back in the country. They'd had plenty of opportunity to address what had happened, with the rest of the family caught up in their own dramas, but Francesca had kept her distance. He hadn't thought it his place to chase her down and discuss how things had changed between them, but that didn't mean she hadn't been on his mind constantly.

If things had been different, if she weren't royalty, and he a member of staff, they might've had a chance of exploring some sort of relationship. Meeting Dan, talking to him, and to Francesca, had made him realise that the unnecessary guilt he'd been carrying was preventing him from having a life of his own. Without the worry of hurting those closest to him, he might have thought about settling down, maybe even having a family. But that was never going to be with Francesca. She'd made that abundantly clear, even if there weren't that huge class divide between them.

'I understand that, but we both agreed that when we got home we'd put London behind us. Sacking me, or restructuring, or whatever you want to call it, doesn't sound like we're doing that. Do you honestly think I'm not capable of doing my job, Francesca?'

'No, I—'

He saw her bottom lip quiver and knew there was a chink in her steely defences. 'I am the one who has been planning every detail of these engagements for you. You know I'll keep you safe. I would give my life for you.'

That much was true. Francesca had come to mean so much more to him than a job, even though nothing could come of these growing feelings he had towards her.

He thought he saw her soften, the tension

ease in her shoulders, but just as quickly she recovered herself. Standing up straighter, tilting her chin into the air in that way that she did when issuing a challenge.

'Fine. You can remain in your position, but my father is counting on me to make a good impression; counting on us to be professional.' The meaning was clear. Francesca was letting him know that there was no room for any more mistakes. Unfortunately, that meant taking their relationship back to the one they'd had before London.

Something that wasn't going to be straightforward when the memories of her touch, and the taste of her, were imprinted on him, body and soul, for ever.

Francesca had tried to put some distance between her and Giovanni by moving him to another security team. In her wisdom, she'd thought it the only way to stop thinking about him so she could focus on her royal duties. She hadn't thought about how that decision would impact on him. He had no family, no partner, no life away from the palace. His job was his life, and she couldn't take it away from him just because her resolve was weak where he was concerned. Because she was worried she wouldn't be able to keep her feelings for him under control.

It had taken a plea from him to make her realise she was being selfish, as well as foolish. Giovanni was the best at what he did. He could read her every move, knew when she was uncomfortable in a situation and needed to get away, or when to back off and take his cue from her. More than all of that, he took her safety extremely seriously. To change the security he provided at the last moment was an unnecessary risk to take. Although the family was popular, there was always a chance of someone launching an attack of some sort, or even just the crowds getting a little too raucous for comfort.

As the limo pulled up outside the school she was visiting today, her stomach was aflutter like the time when she accompanied her parents on her first public engagement. She'd never gone to an event on her own and she was glad now that she at least had Giovanni for support.

'Relax. Your father only wishes you to smile and wave. He's not asking you to get involved in diplomatic matters. Yet.' Giovanni, it seemed, still wasn't above teasing her, and Francesca resisted scolding him for his familiarity again. After all, this had been the nature of their relationship before they'd succumbed to temptation.

'I know. I'm just feeling the pressure of being here alone.' She fidgeted her hands in her lap.

Giovanni reached across the back seat and stilled them with his own. 'You're never alone. I'm always by your side.'

Francesca made the mistake of looking into his eyes, seeing those dark pools express so clearly how much he cared for her. As if realising he'd given away too much, he sat back, and withdrew his touch.

'You know the signal if you want to leave at any time, Your Highness.'

'Yes. I shall take my handkerchief out of my pocket to let you know.' She missed the slightly sarcastic way he used to call her 'Princess'. Even more, the way he used to say her name. Lovingly, in the heat of passion. Exactly why she'd had to put a stop to it.

'Ready?' he asked, before getting out of the car.

'Ready.' She took a deep breath, knowing the circus would begin the moment she stepped out.

Giovanni used to tease her that she didn't know how it felt to walk on solid ground since there was always a red carpet rolled out for her arrival. Now she did, having spent a night running around London in mutilated shoes, thanks to him. This was her first public duty since then, a reminder of her status. And she was worried London had changed who she was for ever. That it would affect her in how she fulfilled her role as future Queen. Today was going to be a test of her mettle, as well as her capabilities in her new role.

Giovanni exited the car first, liaising with the rest of the security team, before opening the car door. Francesca steeled herself and took her time getting out, as demure as possible, so as not to give any waiting photographers a flash of anything she shouldn't.

The cheers of the waiting crowd as she smiled and waved were overwhelming at first, but the touch of Giovanni's hand at her back was as reassuring as the words he whispered in her ear.

'You got this.'

The rest of the security fell into formation around her as she did a walkabout around the playground, where pupils and teachers were lined up behind barriers waiting to see her. She was directed towards a tall, conservatively dressed middle-aged woman hovering nearby, who she was informed was Mrs Bruno, the school principal.

'We're so honoured to have you here, Your Highness.' The woman curtseyed, though appeared a little off balance.

Francesca was used to people being a little nervous, though none would realise she was often just as anxious that the event went well. Especially today, when she felt particularly under scrutiny in light of her father's absence. There would be those waiting to criticise, deeming her unsuitable to follow in her father's footsteps. Too young, too single, too modern, and likely too female for some dinosaurs. So she didn't want to give them any ammunition against her.

'It's my pleasure. I've heard such wonderful things about your school, but I'm keen to learn more. Perhaps I should just say hello to some of the families first.' It was the cue, not only to the security team, but also her host, about her itinerary.

She knew they didn't like it when she did a walkabout with the crowd, from a safety point of view, but she thought it necessary. When people made such an effort to come and see her, it would be arrogant and amiss of her not to acknowledge that.

'Oh, yes, they'll love that. The children have prepared a little something for you too.' Mrs Bruno looked delighted that Francesca was willing to do more than a quick stop. No doubt it would earn her some brownie points with the children and parents too.

'How lovely. Why don't you introduce me to some of the parents and children?' She invited the principal to walk alongside her as they approached the expectant crowd.

Giovanni made sure he was between her and the public, ready to step in if necessary if things got a little out of hand. Not that there was any cause for concern. As Mrs Bruno made introductions to the parents and families, they were very respectful. Most wanting to shake her hand and say hello. There were a few wanting to take selfies, but, as instructed by Giovanni, she wasn't to lean into the person taking them. According to him, this new trend was a security nightmare. She understood that such close contact with strangers was risky, but she doubted anyone here had reason to want to hurt her.

As they were coming to the end of their mini tour, a little girl in her mother's arms handed her a posy of wildflowers.

'Chiara picked those herself,' the mother told her.

Francesca was touched by the gesture, even though Giovanni probably wouldn't recommend taking gifts from strangers. He saw danger everywhere, where she saw only a little girl who wanted to give her a present. Francesca certainly wasn't going to upset her by refusing it. 'Well, Chiara, thank you very much. They're beautiful.'

'Just like you. I like your pink dress and your pretty princess hair,' Chiara said shyly, her head partially buried in her mother's shoulder.

'Thank you.' Francesca reached up and pulled out one of the crystal pins decorating her French chignon. She tucked it into the little girl's blonde ponytail. 'Now you've got pretty princess hair too.'

'When I grow up, I want to be just like you,' Chiara told her.

What should have been taken as a compliment managed to chill Francesca's blood. She thought of this beautiful little girl and the future that lay ahead for her and compared it to the life Francesca had mapped out for her. Whilst she had no control over what happened to her, she didn't want anyone else to fall into the trap of trying to live up to impossible expectations. She wasn't going to perpetuate that myth that a child could only be loved if she was perfect.

'You just be you, Chiara. That's enough.' It took a lot to stop her voice from cracking. Wishing someone had told her the same at that age and saved her a lot of heartache.

'Thank you for everything. It's very brave and kind of you to take the time with everyone.' Chiara's mother shook her hand and Francesca managed a shaky smile before walking away.

Brave. It wasn't a title she thought she deserved. She'd never fought for anything in her life. Not even herself. Letting fear and other people's expectations rule over her. It wasn't something she'd want for any of the children here. Yet, she'd accepted it for herself. Just once she wanted to do something deserving of that description. If only for a little while.

It made her think of what she had with Giovanni. What she wanted with him. How she hadn't fought for him when being with him was the one thing she truly wanted in her life. For however long they could have together.

Although they might not have for ever, she would never forgive herself if she didn't try.

She needed to be brave enough to be with him in any capacity she could.

If he still wanted her.

The entourage carried on into the school where she met staff and was invited to sit as guest of honour as the choir sang the national anthem. Something that brought a tear to her eye for many reasons. Including the knowledge that one day she would be the monarch the children were singing about.

She listened as the little ones sang their hearts out, watched the parents beaming with pride, and felt a pang for that simple life. One in which she would have a loving husband by her side, watching their child perform, where nothing in the world was more important than her family's happiness. A dream beyond possibility because she'd been born into royalty. The only time she'd felt normal, that this kind of life was available to her, had been in London. With Giovanni.

She wanted to capture that feeling all over again.

When Francesca got back into the car, she was positively buzzing with adrenaline. The smile on her face as she waved goodbye to the children a genuine display of happiness, as opposed to the one she'd worn when she'd first set foot in the playground. Giovanni was simply relieved she was still in one piece.

'You took some risks there today.' Perhaps he was speaking out of turn, but he wouldn't be doing his job properly if he didn't warn her about the dangers of getting too close to the general public.

And, okay, he worried more about her these days. Not just because she was undertaking more royal duties in place of her father.

'Shush. They're just children. Were you worried that little girl was going to stab me to death with my hairpin?' She was mocking his concern, but that wasn't what was bothering him. In future she was going to be in more of these situations than ever, and she had to take some accountability. Otherwise, the consequences would likely kill him too.

As she reached up to adjust her hair, he shot a hand out to grab hers. 'I'm serious, Francesca. I don't want you to get hurt on my watch.'

'Do you care about me that much?' Her eyes blazed with a fire that had been missing since their night in London.

'You know I do.' They were both aware he wasn't talking about his loyalty to her in a professional way, the blacked-out back seat of the car now filled with a tension he hadn't felt since their time alone in the city.

'So what are you going to do about it?' There was the chin tilt: the challenge for him to act on those feelings he'd been trying to keep at bay for days, for her sake as much as his own.

In the end, he was only human.

'This.' He lunged forward, wound his fingers in her hair and pulled her into a hard kiss. If he'd expected it to shock her into backing away before they repeated past mistakes, he'd underestimated the strength of her need for this too.

That spark reignited, passion soon flared dangerously into an inferno, Giovanni's need for her overriding all common sense once more. Their bodies clung together like long-distance lovers finally reunited after years apart, rather than two people who'd tried to avoid each other for mere days out of self-preservation.

It was only when the car came to a stop that they were thrown back into reality.

'We're back at the palace.' Giovanni had only just said the words when the staff were at the door, readying themselves for the Princess's arrival.

He looked at Francesca, for some clarification of what she wanted, what she expected from him. Braced himself for another 'We made a mistake, this won't happen again' speech.

She leaned her hands on his knees, bent forward so he had a clear view down the front of her dress, and whispered, 'My parents are away, Isabella is busy with Rowan, and I can send the staff away.'

The implication was very clear. Enough that she didn't even wait for a response, getting out of the car and walking into the palace with her head held high.

Giovanni smiled. Despite all the complications that would surely follow, they both knew he was going to follow her in there. She had his heart, and hopefully soon other parts of him, in the palm of her hand.

By the time he'd reached her bedroom, Francesca had already dismissed the rest of the security team and her personal assistant. She was waiting in the doorway for him, unpinning her hair so it fell in dark waves around her shoulders. As he stood in the hallway he knew this was the last chance for him to walk away. Once he crossed that threshold, they couldn't use the same excuse they'd used in London. This wasn't a one-night fling, something that they could claim was simply exploring the freedom of her anonymity. It was a conscious decision to be together, and at some point they were going to have to acknowledge what that meant. For the future, for his position at the palace, and for them.

However, right now, he simply couldn't seem to stop himself from walking into that danger. Drawn to her like a moth to a flame; unable to resist the beauty, but knowing he'd get burned.

'Francesca—'

She put a finger to his lips, stopping him from uttering another word. 'Before you do the whole "Are you sure? Isn't this a bad idea?" speech, the answer is yes to both. But I don't want to think about anything right now. I've done too much of that these past days. Thinking, worrying, planning…it all gets a bit much. When I'm with you I just want to feel good. And if there's one thing I'm sure of, it's that you know how to do that.'

It wasn't a glowing indictment of how she felt about him, more about what he could do for her, but in that moment he didn't care. He wanted her, and perhaps it was better if at least one of them was only interested in the physical side of things. It might just keep her safer than everyone else who'd got close to him.

As per instruction, he didn't open his mouth to speak, but put it to better use. Lips on Francesca's, he backed her into the room and closed the door behind them. From the moment she'd shown her nerves in the car, he'd wanted to kiss her, hold her. Despite the numerous breaches of security protocol on the visit, it had only made her more attractive in his eyes. Her kindness and patience with the children, and everyone else, showed what a great queen she was going to make. As well as a fabulous mother.

His heart ached that she was going to go on to have a family with someone else. A man who might fit socially, but would never know her the way he did. Having a family wasn't anything he'd even dreamed he could have, but being around Francesca, seeing her with the children, made him want it all. With her. For now, though, he'd have to simply settle for being with her.

This time they didn't need a seduction scene, both knowing what they wanted. As their mouths mashed together, they made their way over to the large four-poster bed in the middle of the room. Stripping off their clothes as they went. Giovanni only stopping briefly to find a condom and put it on before joining Francesca, who was lying naked waiting for him. The sight of her alone strengthening his already flourishing arousal.

Francesca, apparently in as much of a hurry as he was to get carnally reacquainted, pulling him on top of her. Giovanni entered her quickly, and easily. Both of their bodies primed for this moment from the first time they'd given in to temptation.

'I've thought of this every minute since we landed back on Monterossa.' Francesca gasped as he drove himself inside her. The admission spurring his pace in that race to find mutual satisfaction.

'How did we manage to wait so long?' The time they'd spent apart seemed a waste. Regardless that they'd both been trying to do the right thing. Putting aside their desires to prioritise their roles at the palace.

'Sheer stubbornness,' she suggested, arching her back and offering up her nipples for his attention.

Giovanni obliged, sucking hard on the sweet pink tips as their bodies rocked violently together. Francesca's breath was already becoming increasingly ragged, her moans of satisfaction getting higher, and louder. Watching her come to climax at his behest was a privilege he was getting too used to. Knowing he could make her feel this way, that she enjoyed him as much as he did her, urging him on to reach that pinnacle with her. Until their cries of ecstasy rang out around the room. Thank goodness she'd dismissed the staff, or they would've been the talk of the palace, and likely beyond. It seemed playing with fire was their particular kink.

CHAPTER NINE

'I MISSED THIS.' Francesca threaded her fingers through Giovanni's, lifting their hands up so she could see them. Proof that this was real and not just another one of her erotic dreams.

'Me too.' Giovanni rolled over on the bed and kissed her cheek.

'I've been thinking…' She turned to stare into those beautiful dark eyes, which she apparently couldn't resist, along with the rest of him.

'Hmm…' His sleepy response stirred that ache inside her all over again, despite her body being sated only moments ago.

He had that effect on her. Bringing her body alive at the mere sound and sight of him. Ruining her for any other man who could never hope to do the same. The idea of marriage even more of a prison to her now when she knew she could never feel this way about her future husband.

The reason why she was about to suggest something very un-queen-like. 'Clearly, we can't stay away from one another.'

'Clearly.' To prove the point, Giovanni was back, nibbling at the skin on her neck, his hand roaming her naked body again.

'I thought perhaps we could continue to see each other, in private.' Now she had his attention.

Giovanni sat bolt upright. 'How would that work?'

She'd been thinking about it a lot in that ride back in the car, trying to find some way of keeping him in her life in more than a professional way, without causing a drama. In the end, she'd come up with the idea of a casual arrangement.

'Sleeping together in private, yet outwardly maintaining that professional façade, seems like having the best of both worlds to me. Though of course it will mean having to keep our hands off each other in the car, and anywhere else we could be seen. Any physical contact will have to be kept behind a closed bedroom door.'

'Is that really what you want?' He held her gaze, as though willing her to say what was really in her heart.

There was no point when they couldn't be together properly. No one at the palace would be happy about the match, and she didn't want to start her reign on a bad note when the time came. She and Giovanni would burn themselves out eventually and it would cause a lot of unnecessary worry and scandal to go public. This passion between them couldn't last for ever. One day she would have to marry someone suitable, and she'd have her duties to occupy her every waking moment.

Besides, he'd made it clear he wasn't in the market for a serious relationship anyway. At least this way they'd be able to reap the benefits of a no-strings arrangement without anyone getting hurt. And she'd have some very pleasant memories and experiences to cling to when she did finally marry someone suitable as a husband to a queen. Someone who could never make her feel the way Giovanni did.

'Yes,' she lied. He might not agree if he thought she had any feelings for him other than the ones he stirred in the bedroom.

'And how long will this arrangement last?' He cocked an eyebrow at her as though he didn't believe she was actually proposing this. Francesca supposed it was out of character for someone who always played by the rules, but once London had unleashed that wild side of her character it was difficult to keep it hidden. Since Giovanni had been the only one to see that version of her, the real Francesca, it seemed apt that he should be the one to reap the benefits of her too.

'Until any future engagement. Or before, if either of us decide we're no longer content with the arrangement.' Francesca didn't imagine she'd get bored of having Giovanni in her bed, but there might come a time when it got too risky, or one of them met someone else they were better suited to. The idea of him hooking up with another woman who could give him a normal life, the one thing she couldn't, was already hurting her heart. If she was going to really enjoy this, she had to get any feelings for him out of the game and focus on the physical aspect of their relationship.

Francesca was surprised when he hesitated. Here she was, offering him sex on a plate, with no complications. Well, as long as they didn't get caught, in which case they'd have some serious explaining to do.

'And you think we can do that? Sex without getting involved or affecting our lives here?' He was wearing his serious face now. The one she usually saw when he was talking about her personal security. She supposed in a way he was talking about that, even if he didn't know it. It was inevitable that she'd get hurt at some point when it all ended, but that was going to happen now regardless of how or when things ended between them. She was already emotionally invested. He just didn't need to know that.

'I don't see why not. If we're careful.' She swallowed down the lie. If this was going to work she was going to have to smother her feelings. At least she'd had years of practice in that area.

'Okay.' He nodded.

'Okay?' She was a little deflated by his reaction. It wasn't exactly in keeping with the nature of an illicit affair when he didn't seem that bothered to be part of it.

Just as she was about to backtrack, pretend it wasn't a big deal if he didn't want to be a part of this, Giovanni rolled over.

'Okay. I'll be your dirty little secret. For now.' He kissed her, adding to the frisson of excitement already bringing her out in goosebumps at the thought of continuing this fling for the foreseeable future.

He was more than her dirty little secret, he was where she could be herself, do what she wanted. Be free. She was expected to marry, to produce heirs, and be a good little queen, but perhaps that freedom had awakened something in her. That need to control her own life, or at least have a say in it. A strong queen would be able to make her own decisions. Perhaps she'd never marry at all…

'Your father wants to see you in his study.' Francesca's mother approached her in the palace gardens where she'd gone for a stroll to clear her head.

It had been a couple of weeks since she and Giovanni had embarked on their casual fling, and her parents had now returned from their trip. Keeping their relationship secret was becoming trickier. Although that also made the time they did spend together all the more exciting. Which was part of the problem. She was enjoying being with Giovanni a little too much, and perhaps her parents had noticed.

'Why?' Her mother hadn't given anything away, and Francesca would prefer to be prepared if she was about to get a grilling about her love life.

'You'd better speak to him.'

'Okay.' Dread pitted in her stomach. If she and Giovanni had been caught out, there was going to be hell to pay. Not only had they been indiscreet, but her parents would be disappointed, and disapproving, in her choice of partner.

They liked Giovanni well enough, but, as a commoner, he wouldn't be deemed suitable as the husband of the future Queen. She'd known all of this going into the relationship, but somehow her libido had taken over from that usual need to do the right thing. It had felt good at the time, but now she was sure she was about to pay a heavy cost. There was no way Giovanni would remain employed at the palace after this.

She took her time walking back into the palace, her steps echoing around the hallway and marking every move closer to the possible end of her relationship with Giovanni. It was tempting to turn and run. To grab him on the way out and go and hide away somewhere where no one knew them. Maybe even London. Just so she could keep him in her life. She'd already been thinking about how close they'd grown over these past weeks and how she was ever going to move back into her public role without him to bolster her confidence, physically and mentally. This was too soon.

'You wanted to see me, Father?' She put on that calm demeanour expected of her during all of her other royal duties, regardless of her stomach doing the fandango.

'Yes, Francesca. Sit.' He gestured at the chair on the other side of his desk whilst he carried on with the paperwork at hand.

'If this is a bad time I can come back later.' Sitting here listening to the loud tick of the grandfather clock in the corner wasn't helping her nerves.

'No. I just have to sign a few of these letters. That's the thing about taking time off. It's all still waiting for you when you come back.' Another of his little nuggets of advice about running a country he liked to drop into conversation every now and then. It seemed there was no area of her life she could enjoy without the heavy weight of responsibility hanging around her neck.

No wonder she liked time away from it all with Giovanni. He was an escape from everything for her. Though she'd come to realise he meant more to her than that. He was the man she wanted by her side no matter where she ended up in life, regardless that it was impossible. Giovanni believed in her more than anyone, probably even more than she did. He brought out the best in her. The woman she wished she could be in public, as well as in private with him.

A few minutes of her father scratching his fountain pen on a mountain of papers, then he sat up and gave her his full attention. 'Right. We need to talk about your actions whilst I and your mother were out of the country.'

Francesca was regretting the chicken pesto pasta she'd had for lunch. 'Oh?'

She batted her eyes innocently, all the while images of everything she and Giovanni had done in her bedroom these past weeks playing an erotic movie in her head.

'Yes, your mother and I have had a chance to speak to the aides and security who've accompanied you on your engagements, and we've seen some of the footage filmed on your visits.'

Oh, please don't let anyone have taken any snaps of me and Giovanni snogging in the back of the car like two horny teens at a drive-in!

'You shouldn't believe everything you hear, or see.' She was trying to decide whether to brazen it out or just come clean. Neither option holding any appeal at the moment.

'Well, we thought you were the happiest we'd seen you look in a long time. I know everyone has felt the strain with my health problems, and uncertainty about the future. No one more than you, I expect. But you've obviously found a coping strategy.'

Apparently her parents were more open-minded than she'd ever realised. Giovanni was many things to her, but she'd never thought of him as a coping strategy. She supposed he was in a way. Was her father actually suggesting that they keep on their illicit bedroom antics if it kept her happy in her work?

'And—and you and Mother are happy for me to continue?'

'Most definitely. It will make life easier for us too.'

That lead weight began to lift, making her feel lighter than she had since her mother had come to fetch her. 'I'm so glad. I didn't know how to bring this up with you. It will of course bring us some challenges with the general public, but I hope when they see I'm still capable of doing the job, I'll win them over.'

This was more than she could ever have hoped. If her parents were accepting of her relationship with Giovanni, perhaps they could really try and make a go of it. It wasn't going to be easy, and she still had to find out the strength of his feelings, and if they went beyond the bedroom door. But she thought they made a good team. With her father's blessing, she was sure the country would soon get behind them as a couple too.

'Exactly what we think too. Your mother wasn't sure if you were ready to take on more responsibilities just yet, but I think you've more than proven yourself capable.' Her father was smiling as though a great weight had been lifted from his shoulders too, but Francesca had a niggling feeling that they weren't on the same page.

'Capable of what?' Although her last relationship had ended badly, she wasn't sure even the royal family needed to be vetted publicly before getting involved with someone else.

The King frowned. 'Taking on more royal duties on a more permanent basis. I'm not planning on abdicating, but I do think that for the sake of my health I should scale down the number of public engagements I undertake. As next in line, you would be expected to take on most of the ones I can no longer do. Of course, your sister will attend some of the low-key events, but you might have to attend some of the more…diplomatic meetings if I'm unable to be there.'

That brief moment of happiness quickly evaporated. Instead of having her relationship with Giovanni out in the open, she found herself agreeing to burying herself further under the burden of royal life. Something that would surely leave less time and privacy for her to be with him.

Not that she could tell her father any of this now. He was still recovering from his illness, and he needed the reassurance that she would be there to take up the slack. Neither of her parents needed the added stress of her telling them that she was beginning to doubt she even wanted to be Queen. Or that she was sleeping with her bodyguard.

Especially not on the back of Isabella's revelations. They were lucky that their mother and father had held their tempers upon hearing about their escape into the city, and Isabella and Rowan's brush with the press. Telling them any more bad news would be testing their limits, and goodness knew she didn't want the added responsibility of making her father even more ill with stress.

So she did what was expected of her, and smiled and nodded. 'I will do whatever you need from me, Father.'

After all, she was always the dutiful daughter.

Giovanni had been looking forward to spending some alone time with Francesca all day.

They had to be careful when they were out and about, and when they were around other staff. More so, now her parents were back in residence. It wasn't easy getting privacy when there was so much more security on site for the King and Queen. He'd had to resort to sneaking about the hallways at night, ducking behind pillars when he heard someone coming, waiting for the all-clear from Francesca to bundle into her room. One night he'd even had to hide out on the balcony stark naked when Isabella had unexpectedly come to her room, with Francesca hurriedly kicking his clothes under her bed.

Their passionate, exciting love affair had become more of a bawdy sex comedy.

They couldn't carry on like this long term. As much as he wanted to carry on seeing her, the more they engaged in this behaviour, the sooner they'd get caught out. With the likely outcome that he'd get fired, and never see her again. One of those things he knew he couldn't bear. He could always get another job, but he'd come to realise there would never be another Francesca for him. If her father found out from someone else that they'd been seeing each other, the fallout was going to be huge. Giovanni didn't want this becoming a self-fulfilling prophecy, with Francesca getting hurt, if it could be avoided.

He knew he wasn't good enough for her, but that didn't mean he didn't have feelings for her. Before he could decide what he wanted to do, he needed to know if this was nothing more to her than the casual hook-up they'd intended it to be. If so, there was a chance they could go back to the lives they'd had before London, before they'd let their defences down and got to know each other outside the palace walls. Although, if she did have feelings for him in return, he didn't know where that left them. If they came clean to her parents, would they, or the rest of the country, accept him as a partner to the future Queen? Would Francesca even want that, when she'd been so eager to please everyone she'd almost married someone she didn't love?

Tonight, they might have to do more talking than kissing.

The one good thing about a carefully regimented royal household was that he knew the schedule. When security took their breaks, when the next shift arrived, so he could slip through to Francesca's room virtually unseen except for those unplanned trips the family took to the bathroom or kitchen when there was a risk he'd be spotted. Thankfully, tonight was one of the occasions where everything went to plan. He hoped it was a sign of things to come.

As had become their custom, he knocked lightly three times on her door to let her know he was there. Within seconds, she'd opened it and practically dragged him inside.

'You're just what I need right now,' she said, pushing him up against the closed door and kissing him as though she hadn't seen him in years.

Normally, he wouldn't have an issue with her taking control. He was all about equal opportunities, especially in the bedroom. Tonight, however, he'd hoped they could have something more meaningful. He wanted them to talk about the future, and if they had one together.

Not that she was making it easy for him to think, never mind talk, when she was already stripping off his jacket and undoing his tie.

'I heard your father called you in for a private chat today.' There wasn't much that happened here that he didn't know about. It was his job to plan for all eventualities concerning the Princess's safety. A conflict of interests, of course, given their current relationship, but useful for him to know small details about these things, which might involve him to some degree.

The moment he said anything about it, he regretted it. Francesca's good mood immediately faltering. 'Can we not talk about it?'

It went against all his instincts to pause their nightly passionate tryst when it was the highlight of his day, but her reluctance told him something important had happened in that private meeting.

'You can tell me.' He stroked her hair and kissed her softly on the lips. If there was a chance of them having more of a relationship, then they needed to open up to one another for support.

Francesca heaved out a sigh that seemed to have come all the way up from the soles of her bare feet. 'He wants me to take on some more of his official duties on a permanent basis.'

Giovanni could see why that would be vexing for her, but didn't explain her reluctance to talk about it. 'Surely that was to be expected, given his health issues, and your increased workload lately.'

Seduction set aside for now, Francesca paced the room. Eventually collapsing onto the edge of the bed. 'I just… I thought, by the way that he was talking, that he and my mother knew about us. That they were happy for us.'

'I don't understand. How? Why?' It didn't make any sense to him why she would've assumed that the King knew about them, or why she would have preferred that conversation to one about her work. He would've thought that if their relationship had come to light then all hell would have broken loose. With him getting the roasting.

Francesca threw herself back dramatically onto the bed. 'He said I was the happiest I'd looked in ages and he was glad. That I should keep doing more of what I was doing. I assumed he was giving his blessing for us to be together.'

'Okay. And that's a good thing because...?' He closed the distance between them and sat down beside her. If she was saying what he thought she was, he was going to need to be sitting down to deal with this.

'Because I thought that meant we could keep on seeing each other, minus the sneaking about. Like a normal couple.'

'You know we could never be that.' He smiled and threaded his fingers through hers. The one act of solidarity they dared to do in the daytime when they were sure no one was watching. Their 'thing'.

She wasn't declaring her undying love for him, but at least she was letting him know he meant more to her than merely a sex buddy. That was all that he wanted, wasn't it? To know his feelings for her were reciprocated?

Yet it meant by having a deeper connection it was going to be that much more painful when they were forced to part. Their feelings could never change their circumstances, and he was going to have to face that fact. He couldn't be any more than a fling or it would cost her her crown. That would devastate her, and was exactly the reason he'd fought his feelings for her for so long. He never wanted her to get hurt.

Another sigh. 'I know. It doesn't matter now. I'm not going to upset everyone by saying how I really feel.' She was smiling, but he knew her well enough to know that it did matter. The more she acted the perfect princess, the more she'd grow to resent it.

'You know you can talk to me.' She'd opened up in London about her troubles, and though they weren't supposed to get emotions involved these days, he knew they were beyond that now.

He'd wanted to know that she felt something

for him beyond the physical, but now it was real, he had to face the fact that there would be consequences for her if they acted on it. He cared too much for her to let that happen.

'I don't want to talk, Giovanni.' Francesca grabbed the front of his shirt and pulled him into a long, sensual kiss. As though she was trying to express how she felt without actually saying the words. Probably for the best in the circumstances. Then he could pretend that there weren't going to be repercussions if they gave into temptation again.

She set about unbuttoning him, undoing his belt, and he realised he didn't want to do any talking either after all. That meant a conversation he wasn't ready to have just yet. A realisation that this was probably coming to an end. They couldn't be together in the real world because of all the reasons he'd told her about. She was bound to get hurt. Along with her parents, her sister, and everyone else.

'You know what? Neither do I.' They could have one last night together. Before someone got hurt. Unbridled passion. A goodbye that they could remember for ever. Then it was back to real life.

On opposite sides of the palace walls.

CHAPTER TEN

'I SHOULD GO before anyone else gets up.' Giovanni gave her a quick peck on the cheek and made a move to get out of the bed, but Francesca pulled him back down beside her.

'Not yet. Stay and cuddle with me for a while.' She wanted to luxuriate in this land of make believe for a little while longer.

'I've already stayed later than I usually do.' It was a feeble protest as he was already wrapping his arms around her and letting her snuggle into his bare chest.

She didn't want to let him go. Her talk with her father had reminded her of just how far she'd come out of her shell with Giovanni. It was a challenge to go back to that dutiful daughter so eager to please, rather than the woman she was with Giovanni, who did as she pleased for a change. Her time with him was making her want change in her life more than ever, but he'd been right when he'd said they could never be a normal couple. Her future as Queen was something that could never change that fact.

'Wouldn't it be nice to do this every morning? A lie-in, breakfast in bed, and making love without the worry of being found out.'

'Of course, but we'll both get into trouble if we get too complacent. I know how important it is to you to be with someone your parents approve of. As much as they might like me, they'll never approve of me as a suitable match.'

Their little love bubble had burst. Giovanni had given nothing away about his feelings to her, when she'd risked her reputation just to be with him. The scandal of that could have jeopardised her future as part of the royal family and she wouldn't have done that for just anyone.

'I wish I had a normal life, Giovanni.'

There was a soft knock on her door, interrupting Francesca before she was able to tell Giovanni how she felt about him.

'Francesca? Are you awake?' Isabella called through the door.

'Just give me a moment,' she shouted back, then whispering to Giovanni, 'Put your clothes on.'

Francesca pulled on her dressing gown and

belted it to preserve her modesty, whilst he was hopping about on the floor now, trying to get his trousers up.

'I want your opinion on this outfit…' Isabella walked on in and caught them both in a state of undress. 'Giovanni?'

'I should go.' He didn't stick around to plead for Isabella's discretion. Apparently, that was down to Francesca. Instead, he put on his shirt and walked out of the bedroom with the rest of his clothes in his arms. At this point she didn't know where things stood between them.

Isabella blinked at her. 'Did that just happen?'

'It depends what you think happened.' Francesca tried to bring some levity to the moment, knowing there was no way of bluffing her way out of this. It was exactly what it looked like.

'Um, that you and your bodyguard have been having some sort of torrid love affair.'

'Pretty much. Although, given the conversation you interrupted, I'm not sure there's any love involved.' At least not on his part anyway.

Isabella flopped down onto her bed, settling in for story time. 'I thought it was a one-time thing?'

Francesca grimaced. 'Apparently not.'

'After all the grief you gave me about being

with Rowan, you and Giovanni have been risking a scandal right here under everyone's noses?' Isabella had every right to be annoyed at her. She hadn't been a very good sister, or daughter, or princess. It had been selfish of her to ignore everyone else's feelings, but it had also been nice to think of herself for a change. Everything about this thing with Giovanni had been confusing. Conflicting what her head was telling her with what her heart wanted.

'I know. I'm sorry. In my defence, that night we spent looking for you brought us closer together. We haven't been able to stay away from one another since.'

'What are you going to do?'

'That's the million-dollar question, isn't it? We've been seeing each other in secret, but I realise I want more than that.'

'What's stopping you?' It was all so much easier for Isabella. She'd wanted to be with Rowan and just gone for it.

This was it. This was the moment everything was going to hit the fan and she had to decide what road she wanted to take. The one as part of the royal family with all the responsibilities she'd been primed for her whole life, or the one that would see her jeopardise it all to be with Giovanni, who might not love her anyway.

Francesca made a 'pfft' sound. 'I'm not you, Isabella. I can't do as I please and sod the consequences.'

Although she'd been doing more of that lately.

'Nice, Frannie.' Isabella gritted her teeth, her hand clenching the rumpled bed covers.

'You know what I mean. What you do has no real impact on anyone. Whereas I have to be the dutiful daughter, or else the whole monarchy would fall.' A tad overdramatic perhaps, but the royal family needed to be popular. They needed people to look up to them and respect them to have any sort of power. If she messed up, she'd lose that respect and that would be devastating for a future queen. She'd rather disappear into obscurity than deal with the impact a scandalous relationship with her bodyguard would have around her.

'Yes, I'm of no significance at all. Merely a spare princess. A second thought. Someone who has no need to be kept in the loop about any serious matters.' Obviously, Isabella had a bee in her bonnet about her position in the family too.

It had never been her intention to annoy her sister. Simply bad wording and timing on her part.

'You know that's not true, Bella. Trust me,

it's not all puppy dogs and fluffy bunnies being the oldest either.'

'At least you get some respect. I'm just expected to stay in the background and not bother anyone. Not that I've been doing a great job of that either lately.' Isabella picked at the hem of her silk nightie, clearly with things on her mind too.

'But it all worked out for you in the end,' Francesca reminded her, hoping she would forget about Giovanni being half naked in her sister's bedroom, and whatever other grievances had arisen from this chat.

Isabella was undeterred. 'What are you going to do about Giovanni? Is it serious?'

'Not yet. I'd like it to be, but you know it's not possible.'

'Why not? He's a nice guy. The strong, silent type. Unless he's telling us off for going against protocol.'

That made her smile. They'd had their fair share of lectures from him over the years when they'd gone off script. Though they both knew it came from a good place. He cared about them.

'He's a commoner. Not a suitable match for a queen-to-be.' It wasn't a nice thing to say, but she was scrabbling for an explanation other than her unrequited feelings.

'So? This isn't the eighteen hundreds, Francesca. Our mother was an actress, in case you've forgotten.'

'No, I haven't forgotten. She was a Hollywood actress. A well-known name, and the marriage brought them some challenges, don't forget.'

'As all marriages do.'

'Apart from anything else, I'm going to be Queen some day, Isabella. I'll have a responsibility to the throne, not a partner. Giovanni deserves more than being second best.'

Isabella took her by the shoulders. 'Listen, sis. I know you've been under pressure your whole life to be perfect, with focus on the day of your coronation. But you're entitled to have a life too. Otherwise it's going to be a very lonely place up on that throne.'

'That's why I think I'm entertaining the idea of a marriage of convenience. That way we both know where we stand and I won't disappoint anyone else if I prove not to be a good enough wife.'

'Oh, Frannie. You both deserve better than that. You don't have to be perfect. Don't you see? You just have to be yourself for people to love, and I'm pretty sure Giovanni's smitten otherwise he wouldn't be risking his job to be with you.'

It was refreshing to hear a family member say something positive to her when compliments were hard come by lately. This was also the first time she'd been told she didn't have to be perfect. That she was enough. She wondered if it was true. Certainly, Giovanni had seemed to think so in London when she'd been free to drop her public persona. Still, it didn't guarantee that they'd get their fairy-tale ending.

'And if things don't work out? Then I've caused a scandal by hooking up with my bodyguard, and jeopardised my future for nothing.'

'Don't use that as an excuse to not even try. People will get over it. If you want to be with Giovanni, be with him. These things have a way of working themselves out.' Isabella made it all seem so easy. Possible.

'I hope you're right, sis.' Without all the what ifs, and other people's expectations, at the end of the day, she just wanted to be with Giovanni. If only she could be sure he felt the same perhaps they could have dealt with anything that challenged their want to be together.

Isabella hugged her before leaving her alone to process the conversation they'd just had. Along with the revelation that for once she might actually have a chance at love herself. That spark of hope enough to bring tears to her eyes that if she was brave enough, there was a chance she could have it all.

Giovanni made himself presentable in one of the guest bathrooms, wishing he had gone home last night and avoided this scene. Something that hadn't been easy to do when Francesca was lying naked next to him, not having to try too hard to persuade him to stay in bed with her. Which unfortunately had come to bite them both in the backside. He was likely going to have to face a firing squad for his grave offence of debasing the future Queen.

Since the sisters were close, he hoped no one else in the palace would have to find out about the discovery.

Even thinking about the way Isabella had walked in on them made him cringe. Trying to get his clothes on and scarper out of Francesca's room was not becoming of a personal protection officer, nor a man who had any sort of future with her.

This morning had been a wake-up call. This wasn't just about having a relationship that her parents frowned upon and would get over down the line. There was much more at stake than their disapproval. Though that alone would be enough to hurt her. She might claim otherwise, but she was someone who'd spent her life trying to please her parents. And everyone else. There was no way she could live with herself if she upset them.

Since their night in London, all she'd talked about was her freedom, and being normal. But it was a pipe dream. The importance of her status in Monterossa wasn't something she could pretend didn't matter. They'd been fooling themselves with this casual arrangement that a different world was available to them, but in reality it never could be. Even now she was probably taking a verbal battering from her sister, and that was more pain than he'd ever intended to cause her.

Once he felt less exposed, he was about to make his way back to Francesca's room to face the fallout. Only to catch sight of her heading out into the gardens. He followed her past the manicured lawns, resisting the urge to call after her and draw attention from the security detail stationed outside. Instead, he waited until she'd gone past the fountain and taken a seat in the wooden arbour. Where the pink-rose-trimmed trellis sides would afford them some privacy.

'Francesca?' Giovanni spoke quietly so as not to spook her.

'Hey,' she said, turning her tear-stained face towards him.

Seeing Francesca so visibly shaken after the encounter with her sister was a punch to Giovanni's gut, knowing he was the cause.

'Are you okay?'

'I'm fine.' She gave him a wobbly little smile that broke his heart. He knew she was trying to project a strength that she obviously wasn't feeling, just to protect him. To prevent him from shouldering more guilt.

Too late.

'You are not fine,' he gritted out, taking a seat beside her.

'I'm sorry if it seemed as though I was running out on you this morning. I thought you and Isabella needed some time and space to talk alone. Perhaps I should have stayed.' He grimaced, knowing it was entirely down to him for putting her in such a compromising position.

Another sad smile as she shook her head.

'There was no need. Isabella pretty much called me a hypocrite, and she has every right to. I gave her a lot of grief over London, when I've been acting just as inappropriately.'

'We all took risks that night.' He wasn't going to let Francesca take all the blame. They'd all messed up, but by continuing to see her in secret, he'd jeopardised her reputation and her relationship with her family. Not to mention her future as Queen. It was too great a risk to let her take any more.

'I guess.'

'It's something we can't afford to do any more.'

Francesca frowned at him. 'What do you mean?'

'Be realistic, Francesca. It was never going to work between us.' He'd been holding on for too long to the pipe dream that they could be together. It had taken a dose of reality for him to see exactly what was at stake for Francesca, and that wasn't just her reputation. This was a warning, and they were lucky it was only her sister who'd caught them.

It was the reminder he had needed that Francesca was risking her reputation, her relationship with her family, and her future as Queen. All for someone who should have known better than to get close to her. He'd known she'd get hurt. The best he could do now was some damage control before she lost everything because of him.

'This was nothing more than a romantic fantasy that should have stayed in London. Or never happened in the first place.' It broke his heart to say that, when being with Francesca was the best thing that had ever happened to him, but he needed her to think it meant nothing if they were going to sever ties completely.

He wanted to fight for her, but that fear of hurting her overrode everything else. There was no point in delaying the inevitable pain when he'd already caused a row between her and her sister. He would never forgive himself if he caused problems for her with her parents too. Nor would they, or the rest of the country.

At least by accepting the end of the relationship he could prevent the same thing happening to Francesca as had happened to everyone else in his life.

'Well, if that's how you really feel, then I guess there's nothing more to say.'

It wasn't. If he was honest, he knew he'd fallen hard for her, but admitting that wasn't going to help either of them come out of this unscathed. He simply had to push through this pain now, and go and lick his wounds later in private. Then hopefully he'd go back to the life he'd had, with this serving as the perfect reminder as to why he shouldn't get involved with anyone.

'I'm sorry, Francesca. For everything.' Giovanni didn't wait around to hash out everything they'd been through, or what they could have together. He knew exactly what he was walking away from.

Francesca couldn't believe what he was saying to her. He didn't even wait for a response. Simply walked away without looking back. As though she didn't mean anything to him. When she'd just realised how much she wanted him in her life. When she'd dared to hope that she could have that love match she thought was out of reach.

It seemed she'd been right to be wary. She couldn't have everything after all.

Once Giovanni was out of sight, Francesca stood up and walked with her head held high into the palace. She smiled at the members of staff who passed her.

'Francesca? If you're free, we'd like to discuss your upcoming schedule.' Her mother caught her in the corridor.

Francesca's smile faltered a little, as did her voice. 'I just have something to do first. I'll be with you as soon as I can.'

She didn't even stop to make her excuses, her jelly legs threatening to give way soon. They just about held her up until she got to her bedroom door. At which point every part of her stopped pretending she was strong enough to bear the loss of Giovanni, their time together, and the future she'd hoped she'd have with him.

Her body folded onto her bed. The one she'd spent so many nights and mornings in with Giovanni. Where they'd made love, where she'd fallen asleep contentedly in his arms, where she'd realised she'd fallen for him and wanted him in her life long term. And now, the memory she had left here was crying her heart out knowing it hadn't meant anything to him.

Giovanni was gone, and he'd taken a huge chunk of her heart with him.

Deep down she supposed she'd been hoping he'd fight for her. That he'd break down and tell her how much he loved her, proving that she was more important to him than anything.

Now Francesca had to figure out where she went from here. If he wasn't her future, the only thing she had left in her life was her family, and the position she held in it. Perhaps if she put all her focus back where it used to be she wouldn't spend the rest of her days mourning the love she'd lost.

One day she might even get over him.

CHAPTER ELEVEN

'ALESSANDRO, WE NEED to know your plans in advance. You can't just say you're waiting for a call from your friends at eleven o'clock on a Friday night and expect us to keep you safe.' Giovanni didn't like having to give the responsible adult speeches, but sometimes it was necessary. If futile.

'Chill, Gio. It's your job, so just do it.' The minor royal he'd been assigned to since leaving the palace flicked his floppy hair out of his eyes and went back to his phone.

Giovanni gritted his teeth, as he'd been doing these past few weeks for the Princesses' cousin on their father's side. The spoiled teen who attracted a lot of attention because of his online antics, and obvious disdain for protocol, was not as endearing as his past charge. He didn't appreciate him adopting Francesca's nickname for him either.

'That would be easier to do if I knew where

you were going.' And if he didn't simultaneously post his location on social media and cause a scrum of screaming girls that they had to push their way through.

Unlike Francesca, Alessandro adored the attention. Most likely because he didn't have any other purpose in life, yet was still afforded a life of luxury due to his family connections. Francesca didn't have the ego of this self-entitled prat, regardless that she was going to be Queen some day.

Ignoring Giovanni's concern, Alessandro answered an incoming call. 'Yo. Sure. See you there, bro.'

The only thing Giovanni hated more than the teen's ego was his insistence on affecting an accent that related in no way to his privileged background. If he really wanted to be 'one of the people', he could easily give up his wealth and status. Alessandro never would though. It was all an act. Unlike Francesca, who took her royal role seriously.

It still hurt not being with her. Although his new job had taken him away from her, it hadn't managed to stop him thinking about her. Still being part of the royal protection team also meant that he got to hear what was happening at the palace. It appeared his sacrifice hadn't been entirely in vain. Francesca had stayed where she was supposed to be, and by all accounts was taking on more duties as her parents had planned. It had all worked out as it was supposed to. Yet, he was still desperately unhappy. He supposed he always would be when he couldn't be with her but was still in her orbit.

'Let's roll, Gio.' Alessandro grabbed his jacket, still leaving Giovanni in the dark about where they were supposed to be heading.

He'd give anything to be back with Francesca in any capacity, but he knew that just wasn't possible. One thing he did know was that he couldn't stay here. He needed a new start. Somewhere away from the entire royal family. Away from Monterossa altogether.

Preferably where there wasn't an incredibly beautiful princess who'd captured his heart.

'He's going where?' Francesca tried not to freak out in front of her parents, who'd just casually mentioned Giovanni was leaving the country.

Her father dismissed her interest with a wave of his hand. 'I don't know… England, I think. Now, can we tell Mattia you'll be attending the charity ball? He's keen to see you again.'

'I've more important things to think about. I've told you, marriage is not uppermost on my mind at present. I'd rather put my energy into actually helping charities than dressing up to impress people I don't know. That's why I've agreed to be patron of a local women's group that raises money to put less fortunate girls through university, who otherwise couldn't afford to attend.' Since resuming her role as a senior royal, rather than her bodyguard's secret lover, she'd been more assertive in what she wanted to do. Or not do.

She knew it was being with Giovanni, being herself and being honest when she was with him that had prompted her to do the same with her parents. So far, there had been no resistance. It seemed she'd just needed to break out of that mould she'd cast herself in as dutiful daughter and have some confidence in herself to speak up. Things had been better. Except for the huge gap in her life where Giovanni used to be.

She'd thought that once he was gone she'd get back to being her. Now she realised how fundamentally she'd changed just by being with him. And he was leaving the country. She might never see him again. It was a thought that wouldn't go away no matter how much she pretended it didn't matter to her. At least when he'd transferred elsewhere, there had still been a chance she might see him. The fact that he was going back to England without her was like rubbing salt in the very raw wound.

Her parents were still trying to set her up, but no man could hold a candle to Giovanni, no matter how much money or status they had. Suddenly, the thought of him being in London, on the underground, in clubs, or hotel rooms, without her, was unbearable. Being confronted with the possibility of losing him for ever made her want to be that brave princess she knew was inside her. For someone who'd vowed to fight for what she wanted, she'd let him go too easily. She hadn't told him how she felt about him, given him a reason to stay and believe it was worth taking a risk on them.

Francesca only hoped it wasn't too late to stand up for what she wanted. Even if there was a chance of being rejected again.

Giovanni stacked the last of the boxes in the lounge. Not that there were a lot. It was sad that he didn't have much in the way of personal possessions, but he supposed it would make it easier to ship his belongings over to England. This apartment had never really felt like home.

The palace had been more of a home to him. Probably because Francesca had been there. Anywhere with her had felt like home.

He shook his head. It was about time he stopped thinking of her. Especially when he was leaving the country to distance himself from everything associated with her. His old army pal, Dan, had got him a security assignment with a famous young British actor who'd suddenly found himself flavour of the year since starring in a Hollywood blockbuster. Another new start. Though in a city that still held many good memories of her.

He was a lost cause.

The doorbell rang and he climbed over the packaging materials strewn around, and the bags of clothes he was going to donate to charity before he left.

He pulled his wallet out to pay the delivery driver for the Indian meal he'd ordered for his dinner. The last person he'd expected to see when he opened the door was the Princess of Monterossa.

'Francesca? What are you doing here? And where is your security?'

She pulled down the hood of her coat. 'I gave them the slip. I'm surprisingly good at that. Can I come in before someone sees me?'

'Yes. Of course.' Stunned by her arrival, he stood back to let her in. 'Ignore the mess. I'm packing.'

'I heard you were moving. That's why I'm here.'

'Oh?' Since she obviously wasn't here in an official royal capacity, he doubted it was to award him a medal for his service to his country. He had to admit he was intrigued by her appearance when she'd gone to so much trouble to see him. And he wasn't going to deny himself one last chance to see her.

Francesca sat down on the lone hardwood dining chair that was left after he'd got rid of most of his furniture. A symbol of the key difference between them when she was used to nothing less than silks and designer fabrics to rest her backside on.

She cleared her throat, seeming uncharacteristically nervous.

'I can't believe you're going back to London without me.'

Her attempt at a joke would've been funny if it weren't so painful.

'I've been offered a good job. I thought it would do us both good to get some distance between us.' Giovanni didn't need to tell her it was going to take a move to another country to help him forget about her.

'Are you sorry we ever got involved?' Her voice was a whisper, and he could see the sorrow in those big eyes.

But it didn't change anything. He couldn't afford for her to get hurt because of him again.

'No. I'm not sorry about anything we did, but I have to go. It's too painful to be so close to you and not be able to touch you.' Especially now when they were in the same room, and she looked more beautiful than ever.

Her hair was loose around her shoulders, and she'd opted for casual jeans and an off-the-shoulder cream wool jumper. She didn't need personal hairdressers, or expensive couture, or even titles, to be the prettiest princess in the kingdom.

He didn't miss the knitted brow when he admitted his feelings. It was difficult to tell if it was disgust or regret. In the end, he supposed it didn't matter. He was leaving. End of story. There was no happy ever after. Not for him, anyway. Francesca would still be Queen of Monterossa some day, would probably marry and have children, and live the fairy tale at the palace. She deserved it. He just didn't want to be around to witness it.

Francesca got up from her chair. Giovanni held his breath as she approached him and touched his arm. 'Don't go. Or if you must, at least take me with you.'

Now his head was in as much turmoil as the rest of him. He'd made peace with the fact that he wasn't going to see her again. That he was going to have to start his life over again and try to forget about her. He hadn't accounted for her coming last minute to throw all his plans out of the window.

'What are you asking of me, Francesca?' He didn't know what she wanted from him, unless she was simply trying to mess with his head one last time as some sort of revenge for ending things.

'To be with me. I'm done living my life for other people. I want you, Giovanni. I'm finally taking control of my own life and I want you to be part of it whatever happens.'

'I told you from the start you'd only end up getting hurt. I saw how devastated you were when Isabella caught us together. We both know that it would make things impossible for you if we were a couple. It's for the best if I go.' Whilst a huge part of him was thrilled that she felt so strongly for him, and that she was standing up for herself, in the end it didn't matter how they felt about one another. It wouldn't change their circumstances.

She grabbed his other arm now too, trapping him, forcing him to look at her. Not playing fair with her continual touch reminding him of every time they'd been intimate together. 'Isabella already knew about us in London. When you saw me in the garden I was just coming to terms with the fact I'd fallen for you and I was hoping you felt the same. I don't want to be a queen, princess, or anything else, if it means we can't be together. I'll give it all up for you, Giovanni. I'm finally standing up for what I want, and that's you.'

His heart was beating so fast he was dizzy, afraid that this was all a dream when she was saying everything that he wanted to hear. 'Really? This isn't simply a guilty conscience speaking now that you know I have to leave the country before I can even think about getting over you?'

'No. I love you, Giovanni. I was afraid to admit it to myself because I know things aren't going to be easy, but, trust me, I'll do anything if it means we can be together.'

'It's not going to be that easy to simply give everything up that you've ever known. Do you honestly think you can just disappear from public life and the press will lose interest? That's never going to happen. They're still going to want that perfect snapshot of you doing something mundane, comparing it to the life you should be living. I don't want that for you, and I'm sure, deep down, you don't either.'

Whilst he was thrilled that he hadn't been wrong about their chemistry, and he was looking forward to having that future together he'd dreamed of, he knew how much of a sacrifice she'd be making. It would cause her immeasurable pain to leave her family, and her position. It wouldn't be fair to ask that of her.

'I want to be with you, Francesca, but we both know you'll get hurt. I would never do that to you.'

She smiled. 'What about all that stuff about me standing up for myself, and not just going along with what everyone else wants? This is me making my own decisions. I just need to know that you love me.'

Giovanni took her in his arms. 'You know I do.'

Francesca shook her head. 'That's not enough. I need you to say the words.'

'You've become very demanding, Princess.' He threaded his fingers through hers, renewing that bond he'd thought gone for ever.

'Someone told me I need to be brave and say what I want. It's supposed to make life easier for me, apparently.' She shrugged and gave him a bright smile as though the world had been lifted from her shoulders. Not as though she'd just added more to her burden.

'I hope so. I don't want to make your life any more difficult than it already is, Francesca, because I love you very, very much.' He leaned in and kissed her as he'd been longing to do these past weeks.

Though he still had no idea how they were going to make this work.

'Even if I'll no longer be a princess, or even have a job?'

'Always. I'll be here as long as you need me to love and protect you, Francesca.' If she was willing to give up everything so they could be together, he had to let go of everything that had been holding him back too.

He loved Francesca, she loved him, and he knew that was enough for both of them.

EPILOGUE

Two months later

'HOW ARE YOU FEELING?' Francesca turned to Giovanni in the back of the car. This was his first official appearance alongside her, though they'd been spotted out and about over the past weeks.

Thankfully, the public had been won over by the match, with most saying it showed she was a princess of the people, marrying for love, rather than status. Others called it a family tradition. Her parents, too, were happy for them. It seemed they were content just to know she'd found someone who loved her, and they'd always been fond of Giovanni. All that worry she'd harboured over his suitability had been unnecessary. Though these days she didn't care as much about what others thought, not when she was so happy simply being with Giovanni.

He was a loving, supportive presence in her

life, and she knew when the time came for her to step up, he'd be right there with her.

'Inadequate,' he said with a laugh.

It was true, her outfit tonight was a tad OTT for a film premiere, but she wanted to look good next to him. He didn't need a diamanté-encrusted silver sheath dress and bling to make an impact. She was aware their appearance together tonight was going to generate a lot of publicity and she simply wanted to be photo ready. It didn't hurt that Giovanni hadn't been able to keep his hands off her either. That was one part of their lives that hadn't slowed down yet. If anything, they were more passionate than ever, and she hoped that sizzle would last between them for ever.

'You look amazing. As always.' She fixed his black dicky bow and couldn't resist trailing her hands down his fitted shirt, feeling every taut muscle under her hands.

He caught her before she went any further. 'Careful. I don't want to be making headlines for all the wrong reasons in tomorrow's papers.'

He was right, of course, but he looked so good in a tux.

'Mmm, we haven't done it in a car yet. We might have to add that one to the list.' Since the aeroplane incident, they'd confessed to a number of locations where they'd like to engage that risky side of their nature. Careful, naturally, that they wouldn't be seen or compromised in living out any of their fantasies. With Giovanni's helpful knowledge in avoiding detection, so far they'd managed to make love out in the palace gardens and in the pool, without being spotted.

'Not right now, though. I'm desperate for some popcorn.' He was teasing—Giovanni probably didn't even know what film they were going to see—but he was always ready and willing to accompany her wherever she needed to be. He'd even expressed an interest in helping charities too. By becoming a member of the royal family he'd have to give up his security work, but he'd discussed wanting to be involved with ex-military personnel who were dealing with PTSD.

Although both of them were content for now to concentrate on the present, and being together, Francesca hoped one day he would be able to put the past behind him once and for all. Perhaps even make some sort of commitment so she knew exactly the depth of his feelings for her.

Not that she was going to rush him and jeopardise the happiness she'd found with him.

'I suppose we should go in. Remember, smile, and wave. I know it's a new concept for you, but we're here to win people over, not push them away.' She grinned, only half teasing him.

As she reached for the door handle, Giovanni reached out and grabbed her hand.

'Wait,' he said, looking more nervous than she'd ever seen. As a man who'd served in hostile environments with the military, and whose security job meant dealing with danger every day, he was looking pale and uncertain for the first time since she'd known him.

'It'll be okay, Gio. I promise. A couple of minutes on the red carpet, we'll meet the cast, and we can disappear out a side door if you want.' If he was really so ill at the thought of this, she wasn't going to push him. She would never force him to be in a situation that made him uncomfortable.

'No. It's not that.' He fumbled in the inside pocket of his jacket and pulled out a small velvet box.

Francesca swallowed hard, trying not to let her heart persuade her this was what she thought it was.

Giovanni knelt on the floor and opened the box to reveal the most beautiful diamond engagement ring, so big it was dazzling. It must have cost him a fortune, yet she would have been happy with anything as long as the sentiment was the same behind it.

'Princess Francesca, will you do me the very great honour of becoming my wife?' The sweat was breaking on his forehead, his nerves clearly showing, and she appreciated the gesture even more.

'Yes. Yes, I will.' She let him slip the ring perfectly on her finger before he joined her back on the seat and kissed her.

'I love you, Francesca,' he said, which were more important to Francesca than any other four words in the world.

* * * * *

*If you missed the previous story in the
Princesses' Night Out duet
then check out*

How to Win Back a Royal *by Justine Lewis*

*And if you enjoyed this story,
check out these other great reads
from Karin Baine*

Cinderella's Festive Fake Date
Highland Fling with Her Boss
Pregnant Princess at the Altar

All available now!

Harlequin® Reader Service

Enjoyed your book?

Try the perfect subscription for Romance readers and get more great books like this delivered right to your door.

See why over 10+ million readers have tried Harlequin Reader Service.

Start with a Free Welcome Collection with free books and a gift—valued over $20.

Choose any series in print or ebook. See website for details and order today:

TryReaderService.com/subscriptions